SHOOTING STAR

SHOOTING STAR

FREDRICK McKISSACK JR.

ATHENEUM BOOKS FOR YOUNG READERS
NEW YORK LONDON TORONTO SYDNEY

ATHENEUM BOOKS FOR YOUNG READERS

An imprint of Simon & Schuster Children's Publishing Division

1230 Avenue of the Americas, New York, New York 10020

This book is a work of fiction. Any references to historical events, real people, or real

locales are used fictitiously. Other names, characters, places, and incidents are products

of the author's imagination, and any resemblance to actual events or locales or persons,

living or dead, is entirely coincidental.

ATHENEUM BOOKS FOR YOUNG READERS is a registered trademark of Simon & Schuster, Inc.

For information about special discounts for bulk purchases, please contact Simon & Schuster

Special Sales at 1-866-506-1949 or business@simonandschuster.com.

The Simon & Schuster Speakers Bureau can bring authors to your live event. For more

information or to book an event, contact the Simon & Schuster Speakers Bureau at

1-866-248-3049 or visit our website at www.simonspeakers.com.

Also available in an Atheneum Books for Young Readers hardcover edition.

Book design by Mike Rosamilia

The text for this book is set in Hoefler Text.

Manufactured in the United States of America

First Atheneum Books for Young Readers paperback edition September 2010

10 9 8 7 6 5 4 3 2 1

The Library of Congress has cataloged the hardcover edition as follows:

McKissack, Fredrick L., Jr.

Shooting star / Fredrick L. McKissack Jr. — 1st ed.

p. cm.

Summary: Jomo Rogers, a naturally talented athlete, starts taking performance enhancing

drugs in order to be an even better high school football player, but finds his life spinning

out of control as his game improves.

ISBN 978-1-4169-4745-5 (hc)

[1. Football—Fiction. 2. Steroids—Fiction. 3. High schools—Fiction. 4. Schools—Fiction.

5. African Americans—Fiction.] I. Title.

PZ7.M478692 Sh 2009

[Fic]—d22   2008055525

ISBN 978-1-4169-9774-0 (pbk)

ISBN 978-1-4169-9640-8 (eBook)

For Lisa and Mark,
for keeping the faith;
for Caitlyn, for showing the way

SHOOTING STAR

"MOST FOOTBALL PLAYERS ARE TEMPERAMENTAL. THAT'S NINETY PERCENT TEMPER AND TEN PERCENT MENTAL."

—Doug Plank,
former NFL safety

Breathing is a natural process, yet Jomo Rodgers found himself flat on his back trying to remember how to do it. His first spluttering for air felt like someone was driving a spike through his chest.

God, please, he thought.

His current condition, and his simple prayer for salvation, was understandable. He had sprinted twenty yards across the field to try to save a touchdown, only to be crushed by a vicious block delivered by a leviathan-cum-humanoid-now-fabulously-heroic farm boy.

Jomo stared up into the blackness of the cold November night. He could see his breath in the air, frustrated bursts of whiteness blown out in nonrhythmic spurts. The flash of flaring neurons in his frontal lobe caused the familiar illusion of stars bursting around him.

He felt and heard nothing after the initial blow. There was just stillness. Pain works at its own speed. Slowly, then quickly, he grew aware of each stab, throb, and burn.

Jomo took in each new sensation while lying like fresh roadkill. His fingers stung from banging against the leviathan's helmet. He noticed the strangeness of sweat drying on his skin in the frigid air. It had been thirty-three degrees at game time. It was much colder now. Jomo flexed his right ankle, and the pain that surged through him could be quantified as several notches above *Ow* on a pain chart, but below *Morphine cocktail, stat!* His mouthpiece was gone. The salty taste of blood filled his mouth. His lip was busted, and there was a knot on the bottom of his tongue.

"Jomo! Jomo! Dude, you all right?"

Jomo couldn't seem to concentrate on anything outside his own head. It took him a moment to focus. It was Calvin Reynolds, a goofy, wide-eyed, big-butt defensive tackle. Calvin had gotten manhandled on the line, allowing the Madison County running back to fly out of the backfield for a sixty-yard touchdown. But more to the point for Jomo, if Calvin had done his job, Jomo wouldn't be on the ground. At least that was how Jomo saw it.

"Dude, how many fingers am I holding up?" Calvin asked. His fingers were inches from Jomo's face mask.

"Ass . . . hole," Jomo managed in a tone that was less malicious than the curse implied.

Calvin rolled down his index and ring fingers, as well as

his pinky, and then flipped his hand to give Jomo the bird.

"The answer was four," he said, before thumping a knuckle onto the chest plate of Jomo's shoulder pad. "You'll live, bitch."

Calvin and Dr. Hyde—the team's physician who confirmed that Jomo was scrambled but not concussed—lifted Jomo off the turf. It was then that Jomo got a blurry look at the Madison County stadium scoreboard and saw the inevitable lightness of suckitude: fourth quarter, three minutes, thirty-five seconds left in the game; Cranmer 17, Madison County 40. Game over, season over. The team that had had so much promise just got punked big-time in the sectional final.

As he limped to the sidelines, Jomo raised his right hand in acknowledgment of the claps of support from the crowd, the opposing team, and his teammates. His embarrassment kept him from looking up.

"You all right?" he heard.

Jomo lifted his head and grinned at Jayson Caldwell, his best friend, Cranmer's star running back, and the most talented player on the team and possibly in the state. Jayson, who was hobbling over from the bench, had scored Cranmer's only two touchdowns before going out in the middle of the third quarter with a groin strain; they nearly had to tape him to the bench to keep him from trying to get back into the game. Jayson had kept it close until he went out.

Jomo thought how odd it was that Jayson was even in a mood to talk. After losses, Jayson was usually nearly inconsolable. But this game, like the season, had worn everyone out.

Jomo plopped onto the cold metal bench. A team manager gingerly began taping an ice pack to his ankle.

"Damn," Jayson said as he sat down next to him. He started sniffing the air. "Damn, I seriously think he knocked the shit out of you." He smiled and tapped Jomo's shoulder pad. "You a'ight, kid?"

"My hair hurts," Jomo said, which made the trainer chuckle lightly but not loudly.

"I can't help that," the trainer told Jomo.

Jomo nodded and sucked in some cold air and took solace in the fact that he hadn't been seriously injured. He thought about what he'd done right on this night—eleven solo tackles and two tipped passes. But he'd been torched on a long bomb that set up a touchdown and missed a tackle on third-and-long that sustained a scoring drive. From the first day Jomo had put on pads when he was a middle schooler, he had been told that Cranmer football was about results, and the philosophy was fairly binary: Wins are good, losses are bad. While coaches appreciate effort, the final score is all that matters.

"Do you remember them being this big last year?" Jomo asked. "I know I played against some of these guys in freshman football and they weren't that big."

"They either feed them a whole lot or . . . ," Jayson said, before shaping his fingers around an imaginary syringe and plunging it into his arm. Then he waved his hands in the air in disgust.

Juicing, Jomo thought. *Figures.* "Did Coach even do anything when I was lying out there?" Jomo asked.

"Nah," Jayson said. "He was screaming into his headset about how busted the whole play looked. I thought he was going to have a stroke."

Jomo was dumbfounded. Screw him, he decided as he eyed up Coach McPherson, who was still, even as the game was quickly coming to a close, barking out orders.

"Classic," Jomo fumed, remembering Reginald McPherson's concern when Jayson went down. Jomo took a swig of water, swished it around his mouth, and spit out a mixture of blood and water. "I ran my ass off to stop a touchdown. I got blind-sided by some corn-fed guy who probably bench-presses tractors. What do I get? Not a damn thing. No clap. No back slap. No nothing. Screw him!"

"Tried but didn't," Jayson said. "What did you want? A hug and a kiss? You know how he is. Soft as a brick, baby."

"Yeah, well." Jomo sighed. He took another gulp from the water bottle.

"Where's the frickin' punt team, for Pete's sake?" McPherson was snarling, glaring at the team, slamming his play chart to the ground. "We've been four-and-out most the night, so you'd think you all would have this down pat."

Jomo watched the mess before him. It was incomprehensible. McPherson's teams were known for going down swinging. These guys were packing it in and didn't care.

It didn't get better. The line didn't block, and Denny Walsh, normally a good punter, rushed his kick. It was a twenty-yard fluttering duck that rolled out of bounds, setting up Madison for good field position inside Cranmer territory.

One play later Madison scored on a screen play that made Cranmer's players look like they couldn't hit a tackling dummy. McPherson threw up his hands. Madison was pouring it onto Cranmer.

Cranmer's defensive unit jogged off the field, shouting at each other about dogging it, pointing fingers, grabbing jerseys. Then someone let loose a sarcastic laugh. It was as undisciplined a team as Jomo had ever seen.

"My God. It's like watching monkeys fucking footballs! Fucking footballs!" McPherson screamed into his headset before throwing it and kicking it.

People stopped. Jaws dropped. Even the line judge turned to look.

We're now at meltdown, Jomo thought.

As loud and fierce as McPherson was, no one had ever heard him throw an F-bomb. Not on the field. Not on the practice field. Not in locker room or weight room. Not even in intense one-on-one sessions behind closed doors.

"Dawg. Did you . . . ?" Jayson said, leaning into Jomo.

"Yeah, I heard it. He's lost it."

Jomo looked into the crowd. In the seats closest to the field behind the bench were Dr. Campbell—the headmaster—and the trustees. They were a mass of stern looks and pursed lips. He wondered if they'd heard McPherson's bomb, especially Campbell. Cranmer wasn't the uptight place it had been in, say, the 1950s, but there was decorum to follow, and tossing F-bombs out loud was a no-no.

"It's a funeral," Jomo whispered to Jayson. "It's his funeral."

"Coach hasn't won a state title in five years," Jayson said. "We haven't even had a team make it to semi state in four. Getting rolled at sectionals by Madison, shit, he's got to be feeling the pressure."

"I almost feel sorry for him," Jomo said. "Almost."

The football gods were whipping McPherson, he thought. The campaign would end with a 5–5 record, not bad for any other team that started seven sophomores, including at the key positions of quarterback and running back. In fact, with nearly the entire team coming back, most schools would be thrilled about the future. But this was Cranmer, where football was king. This was Cranmer, coached by a legend with eight state titles and double that number of conference championships. This was Cranmer, where the unofficial motto was "Winning *is* the thing."

The crowd started counting down from ten; the game was coming to a merciful end. Jomo watched as McPherson sprinted out to shake hands with the opposing coach, then charged past a TV crew, a radio reporter, and two prep sportswriters and headed for the locker room. He rushed past the headmaster and trustees. He even blew off his wife.

"We are so dead," Jomo said as they and the rest of the team shuffled along off the field. The comment was met with a chorus of groans, sighs, some light blaspheming, and scatological references.

"Boys," began Trey McBride. Jomo rolled his eyes; Jayson looked straight ahead. Trey was the starting quarterback, and he'd been picked off three times. "There comes a time when a man stares at the abyss, and he sees himself . . ."

"Yeah, yeah. He sees himself looking back," Jomo said. "No escape, finds out who he is, blah blah. Yes, we saw that movie in ethics class too."

"No escape from the sustained and deserved ass whippin' we are about to receive," Jayson said as he hobbled toward the locker room.

"Ass whipping deluxe this way, brothers," he added, pointing toward the visitors' locker room door—it was also the girls' locker room, made all the worse by the Madison County's team nickname for its girls' teams, the Lady Golden Beavers.

Jomo was close to making a joke, but he quickly changed his mind when he saw the stone-cold look on McPherson's face.

"In my thirty-two years of coaching the Colonels, I have never seen a team lose in such a GOD awful way!"

Everyone expected the postgame talk to be a loud one. And the spittle flew.

"We lost! They whipped us like dogs, and we looked like dog sh—!"

He kicked a metal trash can against a wall. This was all quite normal. For a loss. Even in a win—Jomo had been confused earlier in the season when McPherson had screamed at them for ten minutes for letting up in the final quarter.

McPherson nearly began to shout again but inexplicably stopped. He looked at the ceiling and let out a loud sigh. Jomo was curious—he'd never seen his coach just stop in mid–butt kicking. He pressed his right thumb and forefinger against the bridge of his nose and closed his eyes. Finally he looked down again and scanned the thirty-five boys assembled. He stared at them as a whole; then his gaze shifted to select players. He caught Jomo's eyes.

Is he having a heart attack? Jomo thought. *A stroke? I think we killed him.*

The room was silent, save for someone blowing out a snot rocket onto the floor. They really hadn't had a shot at winning this game, not against a team picked to play for the state championship down in Indianapolis. But even when a player knows the odds are against him, there's still hope, at least at the beginning of the game, that fortune might smile upon him. Yes, Cranmer had started out well, entering halftime tied at seven, though bad breaks for Madison County rather than great plays by the Colonels kept the game close. But as Madison County took advantage of Cranmer's relative youth, hope slid into despair early in the second half.

Jomo waited to see if McPherson was going to keel over. But what he did next was almost more surprising. McPherson motioned for them to gather in closer, and they instinctively formed a semicircle. He then took a knee on the gray-stained carpeting. He took off his Cranmer baseball cap and drew his hand through his sweat-slicked silver hair.

"Gentlemen," McPherson said. He stopped.

"Boys," he began again, his tone almost fatherly. "What hurt us the most this year?"

It was a rhetorical question.

"Inconsistency," he said as he slapped his hands together.

"That's what killed us. Think about the year. Remember Claremont? They were number five in the state, and everybody had us going down early and hard. I saw some real football that night. We hit them hard on both sides of the ball. I mean slobber-knockin' hits that shook down the ghosts of the Colonels. I couldn't have been more proud of you boys that night. How much did we beat them by that night, Coach Burke?"

"By fourteen, Coach," said Carl Burke, a former player, now the team's offensive coordinator.

"Outstanding! We kicked their rears all the way back to South Bend. I thought we had turned a corner. We were two and two. So what happened the next week?"

Again McPherson looked around the room.

"What happened?" he asked them, raising his voice.

"We lost"—the answer delivered in a low-tone cacophony.

"I can't hear you!" McPherson bellowed.

"We lost!" the team yelled in unison.

"That's right! That's right! And we lost to Delmar Academy."

Now McPherson was on a roll. His rhythm picked up to that of a fire-and-brimstone preacher.

"Delmar! My God, boys, Delmar. There's not a kid on that team who could start for us. They're not fit to hold your jocks. Delmar won one game this year. One! And that was against you. So there you go. You crush one of the best teams in the state, a squad with some bona fide blue-chippers. Then you turn around and blow it against the saddest bunch of pantywaists in the state. So which team are you, gentlemen? I'm mystified as to how this team can be great one game and so bafflingly inept the next."

McPherson then ratcheted up the intensity just a click or two.

"Tonight you got beat by an older team," he said. "I didn't say a better team, because that's not what buried you tonight. What buried you was inconsistent play."

McPherson rose to his feet. He walked to the whiteboard and erased the two unsuccessful adjustments drawn up at half-time. He wrote:

$$HEART + SKILL + PERFECT\ EXECUTION = WINS$$

"For you nonseniors, this time next season, if we don't blow it, you're going to be in a locker room after the sectional final," McPherson said. "Now, if you hate the wretched feeling you're experiencing right now, if it's hard to swallow the bile that's built up in your throat over blowing this season, I suggest you commit this equation to memory. This equation is what is going to deliver this team from mediocrity."

Jomo looked around and saw the words were sinking in.

"Amazing," he whispered. It was a mixture of awe and sarcasm. "A pep talk after a *loss*?"

"Shhh," Jayson hissed.

McPherson pivoted back toward the whiteboard, talking over his shoulder as he wrote in large block letters.

THE FUTURE BEGINS NOW!
ADJUST YOUR ATTITUDE

McPherson turned and looked at the team. The room was eerily calm.

"You saw what the man wrote," Jayson yelled, jumping to his feet.

Jomo looked down and smirked. McPherson stepped back, smiled, and let Jayson take over. The only reason Jayson wasn't wearing a captain's *C* on the back of his helmet was that he was still an underclassman. But now the season was over, and Jomo wondered if this was Jayson's first attempt to establish himself as the team's leader.

Jayson cranked his right arm back and slammed his helmet against the locker. The sound rang out like a shotgun blast.

"Do you have it in you?" Jayson screamed.

Bang! He swung into the locker again.

"Who else has it in them?" he yelled. "If you do, holler 'Colonels!' Let 'em hear it. Let 'em know that we'll be back and it ain't going down the same way next time. Don't go out like some punk!"

One by one, players got up and started chanting "Colonels!" at the top of their lungs. Even the few seniors who had nothing else to give got into it. From the outside it must've sounded like a party. On the inside it was an exorcism, Jomo thought. The taint from this season's failures was being driven out of them.

McPherson's gaze came to rest on Jomo, who clapped and chanted with the rest. Jomo knew instantly that McPherson could tell he wasn't really catching the spirit. He went on and faked it anyway.

But he knew this was where he and Jayson differed, and why Jayson was on the fast track to glory. Sure, he was a good player, and he liked playing, but Jayson was way into being a leader and motivator. He played because he loved it—he was a virtuoso. It was why Jayson had been getting calls, texts, e-mails, and phone calls from college coaches around the country. Not for the first time, Jomo wondered how Jayson was able to get so much more into it than he was. And he wondered whether he'd be getting a few of those calls if he were to put in more effort.

Jomo looked around at each of his chanting teammates and then at McPherson, who watched them appraisingly. Sure, the testosterone-driven moments during games made sense to Jomo. Even the things the guys did to psych themselves up before games—listen to music, bang their helmeted heads together, and shout rally cries—that was all well and good. But it was at moments like these, when emotional outbursts trumped reason—this was when Jomo thought the whole thing was just so much hype.

McPherson was fond of saying that on the farm, what separated hens and hogs was commitment. Hens gave eggs; hogs gave everything. Jayson was a hog's hog. Jomo appreciated that trait in his friend. It wasn't that Jomo didn't want to be a hog, but he always thought of himself as not quite ready for primetime. Despite the fact he was starting, he saw it in the negative: He was playing because someone was injured. During McPherson's long-winded speeches about sacrifice and commitment, Jomo could hear his father telling him ever since he first put on pads in peewee football that this was simply a game.

But he was careful to keep it to himself. One of the few times he and Jayson had had a serious bust-up was back in eighth grade, when Jomo shrugged off a one-point loss to a rival, Ascension, arguing that it wasn't as soul-scarring as Jayson made it out be. When their coaches and teammates finally separated them, they didn't talk for a week.

"Play hard, hang tough" were his father's words the day Jomo made varsity. "But don't lose yourself. Do not get caught up in everybody else's bullshit and madness."

Yet here was a full three minutes of organized chaos before McPherson calmed the team down enough for the Lord's Prayer, a tradition that went back to first game of the first Cranmer team in the late 1890s. "Humble in victory, gracious in defeat," the Colonels said before that prayer. It was a meaningless motto. The Colonels were insufferable in victory and suffered mightily in defeat.

"Our Father, who art in heaven," they all started in unison, hands clasped together in a chain. Jomo, as was his tradition, pretended to care that God cared about Cranmer football.

...

The Colonels traveled in style: a large passenger bus with climate control, comfortable seats, expanded legroom, a teeny-tiny bathroom stall that the linemen hated, and three television monitors. The monitors were mostly used to look at game videos, although sometimes on long trips the coaches would pop in pro and college football highlights to amp players.

Even though it was an hour and a half back to school, the monitors were dark. The bus was quiet. A silent but intense game of hearts was going on in the back of the bus, but most people had tuned into their thoughts or turned on their MP3 players, or were tapping out text messages to each other.

The moon was full and Jomo stared out the window. He made out the dark silhouettes along the Indiana farmland: barns, tractors and combines, tree groves. Jomo had always liked the rural darkness on clear nights, as he stared at the mass of stars in the sky.

He sat next to Jayson, who'd fallen asleep listening to some slow jams on his iPod. Jayson'd turned off his phone after getting three text messages in fifteen minutes from college coaches wanting to know if he was fine. He answered them all. It was getting to the point where Jayson couldn't hold a conversation without someone texting or calling.

He was now leaning into Jomo, not quite snoring, so Jomo gently nudged Jayson back over to his seat. Jayson shifted his body toward the aisle. Jomo glanced over at him, and not for the first time he felt a twinge of awe, and yeah, all right, envy. Jayson was massive. He was the prototypical All-American in the making. Python arms, six-pack abs, oak trees for legs.

Swagger. Jomo wanted it, but Jayson was blessed with lots of it. Jomo caught a glimpse of himself in the window.

And I'm what? Mini-Me?

Jomo had watched his best friend blow up big-time almost the day he'd entered high school. Jayson was already five foot eleven inches and 185 pounds (and expected to grow even more). He was a Superman compared to Jomo's five-foot-eight-inch, 150-pound Jimmy Olsen frame. Jomo hadn't grown an inch—not one stinking inch—since eighth grade. The doctor told him there probably wasn't going to be a growth spurt. Other than his six-foot-two-inch uncle Will, no one on either side of his family tree was taller than five foot ten.

Jomo was just about to shut his eyes when he felt his phone vibrate. It was Trey.

"News. Many T's against McP."

McPherson was losing support from the trustee board.

"Source?" Jomo tapped back.

"Deuce!!!!"

That was Trey's name for his dad, Leonard Andrew St. John McBride II. Deuce—he generally went by Len, not Lenny—was a Cranmer grad, a trustee, and one of McPherson's most ardent supporters. The alumni loved McPherson, but the trustees signed the checks.

"OMFG," Jomo wrote back.

"McP's FU 2 T: priceless," Trey wrote. Another message quickly followed. "Shhh on this."

No duh, Jomo thought. Rumors were going to happen, and listening to gossip was essential. Spreading them, however, was something he rarely did.

"% McP will coach nxt yr?" Jomo typed. The answer came thirty seconds later.

"Very likely. Must go deep in the playoffs next yr."

Before Jomo could respond, Trey texted again.

"Btw, geometry. Pls help?!"

"OK. Call weekend."

Jomo began texting again.

"Mom. We lost. Big! Twisted my ankle. Wish u were here. Love u. Call u tomorrow."

He closed his phone and looked out of the window again. His mom had missed the entire season, he realized. Three months! She'd been gone for three whole months. Well, she'd moved out of the house and into an efficiency apartment months before that. But still, Seattle was twenty-four hundred miles away. Not that he was going to cry about it. But it made him want to pound something—his parents were acting like a pair of two-year-olds.

"Fuck," he blurted out. It wasn't loud enough to be heard by anybody. Yeah, the season had ended badly. But what made it even worse for Jomo was that he didn't have anybody there. His mom was a couple thousand miles away, and his dad was lecturing in Chicago and wouldn't be back until Saturday afternoon. His uncle, who normally caught Jomo's games, was unable to break away from work. Jayson's mom, who was in one of the two supporters' buses chartered by Cranmer, would take him and Jayson out for burgers when they got back, but he'd go home to a dark house. *Sucks to be me,* he thought.

"Rodgers, Coach wants to see you," said Adrian Sims, the defensive coordinator, leaning over Jayson and into Jomo's face.

"Hunh?" Jomo said, cocking his head away from the window.

"Coach wants to talk to you. Now," Sims said, motioning Jomo to move it.

"What's he want with me?"

"What?"

"Did I do something wrong?"

Sims peered over his glasses. He folded his arms.

"I don't know. Did you?"

Jayson stirred a little as Jomo limped over him. Trying not to put too much weight on his right ankle, he shuffled down to McPherson's seat at the front of the bus.

"Coach?" Jomo said.

McPherson was studying some notes in a folder. He nodded and pointed to the seat next to him without looking up. McPherson read for another thirty seconds before closing the folder. He kept his eyes straight ahead.

"You feeling all right, Rodgers?" McPherson asked.

"Yeah. . . . Yes, er, sir, other than my ankle," Jomo said tentatively, wondering where this conversation was headed.

McPherson swung his head around and looked directly at him.

"No, I mean, how do you *feel*?" he asked.

It was the emphasis on "feel" that confused Jomo.

"I feel . . . ," Jomo started. He stopped, realizing his voice had gone all nervy and high. He started again in a lower, calmer voice.

"I feel fine, Coach. Why?"

McPherson shifted in his seat. His entire body was now facing Jomo. His expression was intense.

"Do you think you're a good football player?" McPherson asked, forcing Jomo to make eye contact. Jomo tensed. What kind of question was that? Was this a trick? he wondered.

"I guess so—"

"No guessing, son. You've got to know so. Do you know so?"

It was the first time since Jomo had been named to the varsity squad that McPherson had talked to him this intimately, or called him "son." McPherson had screamed, back slapped, helmet slapped, cajoled, and ridiculed him all season, sometimes all in the same game. So now Jomo didn't know how to act or even what to expect. Therefore, he nodded an unconvincing affirmative.

"The team's biggest problem is inconsistency. However, your problem is commitment," Coach said. "Don't get me wrong. You've played hard this year. Hell, you were supposed to be backup, but when Ferguson broke his leg, I had to start you."

"I wish we hadn't lost Fergie. Maybe we could have—"

McPherson cut him off. He pointed his index finger just a few inches from Jomo's heart.

"There you go again. Ferguson's absence shouldn't matter. You stepped up to the plate when we needed you—most of the time. You ball hawk like a senior—most of the time. At practice you work hard enough—most of the time. You hear a pattern? You're there sometimes, and other times your head is somewhere else."

Jomo pressed himself back against the seat. McPherson then looked out the front windshield.

"Rodgers, the team has an optional early-morning weight-lifting schedule. I saw you at the morning workouts once, maybe twice. When we've made game tapes available to take home, I don't think I saw your name on the sign-up sheet at all."

McPherson paused and narrowed his eyes.

"Ask yourself this question," he said slowly, deliberately. "Could Cranmer have been better if I were more committed? It's a team sport, son, but it begins with your commitment, your desire, your heart."

Jomo stared at the speckled fiberglass floor.

"Son," McPherson said. "Look at me, son."

But he couldn't, not directly in the eyes. So he focused on the bridge of McPherson's nose. Then realized what a wussy move that was, so he forced himself to lock his eyes directly with McPherson's.

"This game is easy hard," McPherson said, his voice suddenly moving toward that of a grandfatherly man offering sage advice. "Do you know what I mean? If you give me a hundred percent, if you give me every ounce of energy and attention, I can make you into a fantastic football player. You're small. Hell, in my day, you would've been just fine. But nowadays, with everybody sucking down supplements or injecting whatever else into their butts, even kickers are as big as linebackers were twenty or thirty years ago. You need to gain some muscle, and it starts in the gym. You give me an hour a day in the gym at least five days a week, and by the time you're a senior, you'll be plenty big and you will be plenty good. You read me, Rodgers?"

"Yes," he said sheepishly.

"Rodgers, you've got to give it all if you want to play big-boy football. Jayson gives it all. You need to model that."

Jomo nodded, but he was thinking something else that he couldn't say. Football was all Jayson had. If it weren't for him tutoring Jayson in geometry and biology, he'd flunk out.

"I'm giving you all the rest of the month off," McPherson said. "But we're getting back to the gym in December. Coach Sims will give you some assignments and instructions. We clear on that?"

"Yes, Coach."

"Dismissed."

Jomo limped back to his seat, climbed over the still-sleeping Jayson. He fell into the seat, banging his ankle against the footrest.

"Dammit!" he grunted.

"What!" Jayson said, waking up.

"My ankle," Jomo said.

"Oh. I thought it was something important," Jayson said. He laughed. Jomo didn't. He sighed loudly, a signal to those who knew him that he was either pissed off or confused or both.

"What are you beefing on now?" Jayson said, fully awake and sitting up straight.

"Do you think I'm a good football player?"

"Does it matter?" Jayson asked.

"Yes. I'm asking you. You've known me since we were, what, in pull-ups. I'm asking you, am I any good?"

"You're not as good as me. . . ."

"This isn't about you." Jomo's voice was a little louder and angrier.

"Damn, what's up your ass?" Jayson snapped back. "Fine, motherfucker, you can play when you want to play."

"What the hell does that mean?"

"It means what it means. You're smart. Figure it out."

"Is this a lovers' spat?" asked Calvin Reynolds, sitting in front of them, trying to be funny.

"Shut up, fat boy," Jomo said.

"What's his problem?" Calvin asked, looking at Jayson.

"I don't know, but maybe you should stay the hell out of this," Jayson said.

Calvin disappeared. Jayson turned back to Jomo.

"Seriously, homes. You need to check yourself. Calvin could kick your ass, no sweat."

Jomo froze for a moment, trying to collect his thoughts.

"So you think I can play."

"Yeah, and if you really cared about football, you'd be better. I know your pops has different expectations for you. But let's suppose that his son is good enough to play big-boy ball—"

"You know how he feels about that," Jomo broke in. "He just goes on and on about how young brothers are taken advantage of by the *system*," he added, making quote marks with his hands when he spit out the word "system."

Jayson guffawed. "I hate when you do that mess with your hands," he said. "Anyway, dude, if you had mad skills, your father would sing a different tune. Plus—and let's face it, and I don't mean no disrespect, because your dad has been like a father to me, but, you know—he's a very bitter brother."

Jomo sighed.

"I mean," Jayson continued, "add all that and the fact that your mom left—"

"Let's not go there, okay?"

"I'm just saying . . ."

"Stop saying," Jomo said, clenching his teeth and jamming his feet hard enough to bend the metal footrest. Jayson stopped talking and put in his earbuds.

Jomo looked out of the window. Back in June his mom was offered a three-year teaching appointment at an art institute in Seattle. His dad could've taken a sabbatical, Jomo knew. He'd seen other professors do it. But his father was too stubborn—he didn't want to hear about it. The more Jomo's mom pressed, the more his father dug his heels in. "You go, then stay gone," his father had said a few days before his mom moved out. *And she did, Dad,* Jomo thought, balling his right hand into a fist. He just wanted to scream. Jomo would've missed Jayson and some friends, but he didn't give a damn about living in some mid-size "family friendly" city in Indiana. But his parents talked, then fought; then ultimatums were thrown, and his mom moved out.

"Jomo," Jayson said, breaking the silence.

"Yeah."

"To answer your question: I don't get sick to my stomach when I watch you playing."

Jomo tried very hard not to smile.

"Do you feel better now, Li'l Jomo?" Jayson continued. "Would you like Daddy to read you a Li'l Bear story? How about *Corduroy*?"

Jomo smirked. "Jackass," he said, lightly jamming his elbow into Jayson's arm.

"Bulldog!" Casey Fitzgerald called out from the bottom of a gulley that formed a bowl with slopes fifteen yards from the center. The bowl was full of wet leaves and tree limbs.

It was dusk. Most of the members of the Cranmer football team—dressed in ratty sweatshirts and sweatpants, some even in shorts—gathered at the deserted south end of Mission Park, which straddled two of the city's wealthiest neighborhoods. It was eight days after their humiliating defeat. There were thirty players standing at one end of the bowl.

"Bulldog," the group boomed back. And then they all dashed as fast as they could down the slope. Casey, a junior linebacker known as Fitzie, spotted Cael Zimmer, the team's kicker, and drilled him to the floor of the bowl with a forearm to the chest.

"Too easy," Cael said, laughing, as Fitzie pulled him up. "Go for the kicker first."

"Bulldog!" Fitzie and Cael howled.

"Bulldog!" the rest shouted.

Before they got to the park, Jayson explained to Jomo that Bulldog was like playing red rover, except the action was far more ferocious. As the only sophomore who had played varsity last year, Jayson had been through the tradition.

"It's kind of like in *Fight Club*," Jayson told him. "First rule of Fight Club: Don't talk about Fight Club."

"What happens?" Jomo asked nervously.

"You'll see."

Bulldog started out with one person at the bottom of the bowl, the rest standing atop one side of it. The man in the center screamed, "Bulldog," the rest replied, and they ran like screaming mad fools down one slope and up the other. The man in the center had one task—take someone out. Drop them as hard as possible. Now there were two in the center, and they would try to take out two more. The game went on until there was no one left to run down the slope.

Jomo survived for a while, bobbing and weaving as best he could. But he was finally taken down with a jersey pull of a tackle by a lumbering Calvin Reynolds.

"Crap, I got caught by you?" Jomo yelped.

"It ain't like you're Jayson, yo," Calvin snapped, before he burst out laughing.

Indeed, Jayson was the last player to get knocked out, and it wasn't easy. He juked, stiff armed, and leaped while most of the team stood and watched. It finally occurred to them that they could gang tackle him, which they did.

As most of them lay there panting, drenched in sweat despite the slightly-below-freezing temperature, Fitzie and another player, Pat Reardon, dashed up the hill and returned moments later, each carrying a box. Dixie cups were passed out.

"What's this for?" Jomo asked Jayson.

"Shhh."

Jomo turned to Trey and pointed at the cup, figuring that Trey would know, as his older brother was on the team. But Trey only shrugged.

Reardon, one of handful of graduating seniors on the team and the team's captain, reminded Jomo of Chris Farley, both in physical stature and comic presence. He reached into a box and pulled out four bottles of Wild Turkey.

"Take enough for a shot," he told the team. "About two fingers . . ."

One kid began measuring with two fingers in the cup.

"Dammit, on the side, you idiot," Reardon yelled, adding, in a mock threatening tone, "Everybody better damn well get two fingers full. No pantywaists."

The bottles were passed around.

"We done?" Reardon said, looking around. "Gentlemen, the tradition of bulldog only has an oral history and goes back to 1962—"

"I thought it was '72," someone blurted out.

"It was '62, Middlebrook, you ignorant bastard," Reardon retorted, pointing at his best friend, Chip Middlebrook.

"That's Mr. Ignorant Bastard to you, sir," Middlebrook roared back, breaking up the team.

"Anyway"—Reardon regained control—"back then, the team met after a losing season and played a game that was part red rover, part kill the man with the football, and all hitting. It is said that they did this as a way of knocking off the demons of the season, the grudges, the bullshit. They called it bulldog. The next year they won state, so they did bulldog again. The Colonels do this every year, win or lose. And after this season, well . . ."

A six-foot-six, 280-pound offensive tackle who was heading off to Dartmouth, Reardon was a tough, thick-necked, red-headed monster with the well-deserved nickname Animal. Jomo had only ever seen him with two emotions—sarcastic and pissed. But now Jomo noticed Reardon was misty-eyed.

"Boys," Reardon continued, pulling himself together. "To the Colonels!"

"Colonels!"

Everyone drank up, some faster than others, and in Jomo's case, it was a gulp. Damn! At first he thought his esophagus was melting. It gave him a shiver. He wanted to spit it out, but that would be social suicide. The warm liquid slid down through to his abdomen—a weird feeling like he'd swallowed something living. Then, for a moment, he wanted to hurl, but he caught the bile backwash before he spewed. And his father drank this stuff all the time! Damn. The few cheap beers Jomo had drunk—Mickey's, Bud Light, PBR—weren't great, but at least they didn't taste like battery acid.

"And now for the team awards," Reardon said, slapping his hands together, an evil grin on his face. And from the other box he pulled out a half dozen cheap participation trophies—each with a placard that had the name of silly awards etched on it. The first one went to Calvin for Fattest End. As Calvin sheepishly got up to get his trophy, a few guys started chanting, "Speech, speech, speech." After a few more award presentations, including Trey getting what seemed to be the coveted "Annual Most Likely to Actually Be Kicked in the Ass by McPherson" award, Jomo was surprised to hear his own name yelled out.

"Jomo Rodgers," Middlebrook called. "Stand your ass up, son."

People clapped and whooped. Jomo had been sitting with

Jayson and Trey on the western slope trying not to shiver from the cold. He slowly got up and brushed leaves off his butt, feeling embarrassed. He looked down into the pit where Reardon and Middlebrook held court.

"Jomo Rodgers, you are the recipient of the 'Damn, If He Was Just a Little Bit Taller, He'd Be a Big-Time Baller' award."

"He's going to be a helluvan intramural football star somewhere." Reardon laughed, motioning Jomo to walk down to get his award. When Jomo didn't move, Reardon added, "No, seriously, dude, you rock." He started clapping and clapping. The rest of the team joined in. "I saw him put the hurt on guys way bigger than him."

"Too bad he bounced off a couple of guys in the meantime," Trey said, guffawing and drawing laughs.

"Speech! Speech!"

Jomo held the award for a moment. It was even engraved with his name. For as long as he could remember, he'd been the smallest and/or youngest in class. Now he was being rewarded for it—Christ Jesus, why?

"Umm, I—," he said faintly.

"Speak up," someone said.

He looked at Trey and Jayson and noticed that they looked embarrassed and amused. *Camaraderie,* he thought. *Bullshit.*

"Ah, thank you, I think," Jomo said, shrugging and struggling to find words. "I hope not to live up to this."

No one laughed. There was an awkward pause.

"Jomo Rodgers, folks, on the big side of impishness. Give 'im a hand," Reardon joked, slapping Jomo on the back.

Jomo rolled his eyes and plopped back down next to Jayson. He wanted to throw the award as far as he could.

"Suddenly you don't have anything to say?" Jayson asked. "'I hope not to live up to this' is the best you can do?"

"Yeah, well . . ."

But before he could answer further, he was saved by the next award being called. He didn't want to go into it with Jayson, but damn, he was tired of taking crap from upperclassmen. He'd proven himself enough this season! He wanted to be taken seriously. He was *going* to be taken seriously. Then he told himself to calm down. He reminded himself that he wouldn't have gotten any award at all if the guys hadn't liked him. He took a deep breath and focused on the next award.

"Jayson Caldwell," Reardon said, with a faux jive voice. "Jayson Caldwell in da house."

Jayson stood.

"You're the recipient of the 'Damn, I Bet That Brother Will Be Playing on Any Given Sunday' award," Reardon said. Jomo was astonished at how reverential Reardon suddenly sounded. "This is about as close as we get to an MVP award," he added.

"For real, dude, you are fucking big-time and we're lucky to have you," Middlebrook concurred, shaking Jayson's hand.

The team clapped and cheered loudly. A few even stood up.

"I ain't got much to say," Jayson began. "We didn't finish like we wanted. I didn't finish like I wanted. But this I promise: With Fitzie leading us, with this team doing what we're capable of, we will finish on top. You can bank that."

"Damn straight," Fitzie called out.

With that, Reardon said the three words they'd wanted to hear for the past hour and a half: "Party at Middlebrook's!"

As Jomo rode in the back of Fitzie's car, crammed between Jayson and Trey, he beat himself up about how lame his "speech" had sounded. He should have said something clever, something cool, something that demanded respect. But he stood there like a freaking moron. And that damn award, the award for not being big enough, was just more proof that no matter how hard he tried, as long as he was on the small side, he would never be more than a pretty good high school football player. If he gained ten pounds, he might attract the interest of a small college. But would that get him what Jayson had? People respected Jayson. And feared him on the field. No one was fearing Winnie the Pooh in a helmet here. He was now even more determined to get into the weight room. His cell rang.

"Hey, Dad," he said. "Yeah, well, come on, I didn't—"

Oh, this was good. He was getting yelled at for not cleaning the bathtub out well enough. He was in the car with his teammates and his father was bitching up a storm over housework.

"I'm sorry it's not to your standards," he said, cupping his hand over the phone. "I'm not getting mouthy." After a pause, he said, "Right now? You want me to come home now? Fine. Yes. Fine. Fine. I'll have to take the bus. You'll come and get me? I'll call you with the address when I get there. Fine. Yes. Bye."

Jomo closed the phone and jammed it into his coat. They'd be partying while he cleaned the tub again. Jesus H. No one said a word until they got to Middlebrook's house. Jomo waited for his father out front, by the gate. He refused to turn around to see if people were looking, laughing at him.

A few minutes later, Jayson walked out of the house and handed Jomo a can of soda.

"Beer?" Jomo joked.

"Puh-lease." Jayson laughed.

"Thanks."

He popped the top and took a long drink, then offered some to Jayson, who waved him off.

"Why is he such a . . . a . . . freakin' . . ." Jomo didn't know what to say.

"Because"—Jayson shrugged—"your dad is wrapped too tight and your mom is gone."

"But that's not my fault," Jomo said.

"Yeah, but you're here at home, and he doesn't know how to be anything else but the Good Dr. Rodgers—"

"Here he comes," Jomo said, cutting Jayson off.

"I'll call you later, man," Jayson said, high-fiving his

friend. "Jomo, just remember that he does love you. He's just screwed up."

At that, Jayson turned and walked back to the party. Jomo opened the car door and got a lecture all the way home.

"Six," Jomo yelled out as he looked at his watch. "A.m."

For Jomo, a notoriously late sleeper and chronic alarm clock abuser, this was an impossibly early hour. It was made worse by the fact that the sun wasn't up, there was frost on the windows, the morning birds sounded tired and joyless, and he would have to make the mile and a half to school on foot.

"I ain't ready for some football," he sang in with a twang that would've made Hank Williams wince. He alternated between a fast walk and quick jog, his backpack of clothes and books adding extra weight. Great cardio, Jayson had told him the night before.

"Yeah, great," Jomo had grumbled. "I've got big lungs to make up for my tiny nuts freezing off."

He'd promised Coach that he'd hit the weights, and if anything, Jomo was trying to follow the advice of his father, his uncle, and his grandfathers, when they were alive—be a man of your word. That was what he'd convinced himself as he'd tried to get to sleep last night, knowing the alarm would go off in six hours.

Even in the dark, Cranmer's main building was impressive. Jomo joked that it looked like a castle—a Gothic three-story brick-and-stone building that stretched for a half block along a well-manicured, tree-lined street. The building was embellished with two smallish corner turrets. The larger turrets—the ones that gave Cranmer's facade its distinctive look—elegantly rose from the center, framing the long front staircase and an enormous front door with the school's name etched into the stone above it. An inscription on the stone walk of the outside entrance read: DISCERE SI CUPIAS INTRA: SALVERE IUBEMUS ("If you wish to learn, enter: We welcome you"). Jomo's father laughed the first time he saw it, because Latin had been phased out of the school twenty years earlier. Still, students knew what it meant, even if, as Jomo often thought, it didn't always ring true.

Overnight, one of the few things left lit was the atrium at the entrance, which contained a large bronze bust of the school's founder, Colonel Barnabas H. W. Chisholm, a retired cavalry officer. Jomo jogged around the building and through the parking lot and stopped in front of the sports complex, a modern-looking glass-and-brick structure that connected the gym with the stadium.

Getting into the building required a code, which Jomo

momentarily forgot. His fingers were freezing by the time he'd punched the correct numbers in. *This is what six a.m. does to a guy,* he thought. When he walked in the weight-room door, he came face-to-face with a tallish woman in red shorts and a white, long-sleeved T-shirt emblazoned with a volleyball and the words "You wish you hit like a girl!" Her red hair, pulled back into a ponytail, was slicked with sweat, and she was patting her glistening face with a white towel. Her legs were about a mile long. Jomo forced himself to look away.

"U-um," he stammered.

"Yes?" she said, throwing the towel near her desk.

"I'm looking for Jerry Makepeace," he said, dropping his bag on the floor. He buried his hands into the pockets of his hoodie and tried not to look as shocked as he felt. But seeing an attractive young woman at Cranmer, especially one in the weight room, *was* a shock.

"I'm Jeri," she said.

"I thought you'd be—," Jomo started.

"A man, right?" she said sternly.

The hair on the back of his neck stood up. Great. He'd pissed her off in record time. He pulled at the liner of his hoodie. She shot him a smile.

"It's short for Jeri," she said, before adding, in a giggling, girly-girl voice, "Do you have a problem with a woman inside the hallowed halls of he-man Cranmer?"

"Wha—no! No."

"I'm just yanking your chain, kid," she said, extending her

hand for a handshake. "Uncle Reg has called me Jeri since I was kid. You're Jomo. At least I hope you are."

"Uncle Reg?" he asked.

Jomo had only heard people call him Coach, Coach McPherson, or Mr. McPherson. Even his wife referred to him as Coach in public. Uncle Reg sounded, well, in an unfamiliar context, as if there were a softer side to the old man.

"Is he your real uncle?"

"No." She smiled. "He's my godfather. He and my dad played high school and college football together, served in the Army at the same time, and for a while coached at the same college."

His stammering continued. "How—how did you, you know, get this gig?"

"Uncle Reg asked me if I'd be interested in doing some strength and conditioning work. I've got a bunch of flabby soccer moms I work with, and he knew that working with athletes is what I've wanted to do since college."

"So . . ."

"Look, Jomo, we don't have a lot of time, so let's save the questions for later. Let's focus on you. Before we get a plan started—and it will be specific to you being a safety—let's measure you for height, weight, body fat. So remove the hoodie—and did you wear shorts?"

Jomo slowly nodded.

"Okay, get out of the warm-ups."

Jomo pulled the hoodie over his head and then stepped

out of the sweatpants. He balled them up under his arm, trying to act nonchalant. Jeri took out calipers and a PDA from her desk. "I need your arms," she said to him.

"Huh?"

"Your arms. I've got to measure them."

"Oh, right, yeah." Jomo finally got it and tossed his warmups on the carpet.

Jeri started pinching bunches of skin and measuring his arms, his legs, even, much to his embarrassment, his abdomen, raising his shirt so she could pinch his baby fat. The horror. The horror. He wondered if she could tell he was sucking his gut in. At least no one else was there in the room with them. But that almost made it worse, because now his mind was wandering *there* for a moment—she was smoking hot, and he was trying not to pop a chubby. Think unsexy thoughts.

"Hop on the scale," she said. The digital readout flashed 152. Jeri continued to calculate, while Jomo waited, thinking about unsexy things.

"BMI looks good for a football player," she told him, breaking the tension.

"Body mass index, right?" Jomo asked.

"I see someone paid attention in P.E."

King Dork smiled and wished he were back at home asleep.

"Are you going to eat those?"

"What?" Jomo asked, looking up from his lunch tray.

"Are you going to eat those saltines?" Fitzie asked.

"Yeah, you can have my crackers." Jomo laughed. "Do you want both?"

"Cool. Thank you." Fitzie sat down beside Jomo.

"By the way, why are you sitting at *our* table?" asked a clearly incredulous Sherman Harper, also known as Brother X or Militant Brother Number One.

"Fitzie can sit here," Jomo said, slapping his teammate on the back. Fitzie was too busy sizing up his crackers to respond.

"Then it's not the Black Table, is it?" Harper replied tersely.

Nearly every day Jomo sat with Jayson at the unofficial Black Table, where the handful of Cranmer's African American students ate lunch as a group mostly out of habit and solidarity tradition. Cranmer's lunch period was broken into two sections to accommodate the five hundred students. There were twenty-eight black students in the school; first lunch hour had ten of them.

Jayson could always be found at the Black Table. Jomo being Jomo, he claimed his right to be a social free agent who bounced between the skaters and alt music/technology geeks (not to be confused with the technology geeks with no sense of music) and some of the cooler debate members who spoke slowly enough to make coherent points. It didn't make Harper, a junior, happy, and he'd been hounding Jomo since his freshmen year about his "Oreo" attitude.

"Dude, how much weight have you lost?" Jomo asked,

ignoring Harper, watching Fitzie pick the salt off the crackers. Apparently, salt added water weight.

"Oh, I'm down to one seventy-five." Fitzie beamed, nibbling on a cracker.

"Yeah, you've got a little Skeletor thing going on with your cheeks," Jayson said.

"I know, it's great. I'm almost at weight," Fitzie said as he bit off and clearly savored every minuscule piece of cracker.

"Hunh?" asked Terry Burrell from across the table. Terry was a quiet and genial freshman who followed Harper around like a puppy. As far as Jomo could tell, "Hunh" was pretty much all the kid would say.

"Wrestling season," Jomo told him.

"That's why I don't wrestle," Jayson followed up.

"Got to get the weight down," Jomo added.

It was kind of crazy when Jomo thought about it. During football season, guys generally ate what they wanted. If some linemen could have unhinged their jaws at a buffet, they would have. It was all in an effort to maintain weight, or even bulk up. But for guys who wrestled, it was amazing how fast some of them would lose weight—some seemed almost masochistic—purging or starving.

"If they were women, they'd all be in counseling," Jomo had said when he'd first heard about it freshman year. He came close to getting his scrawny self lit up by a junior who overheard his remark.

Fitzie was now wetting his finger and pressing it against

his plate, getting up every last crumb. Jomo felt for him. Fitzie tipped the scales at 190 during the season, then had to scramble to lose 15 pounds in a matter of weeks to wrestle in a class that was suitable for his competing for a state title. He was a bout shy of winning it last year, so the pressure was on.

"Fitzgerald, you're one of the richest white boys up in here, and here you are begging for crackers," Sherman cracked. "You ever consider fen-phen?"

"Hell no," Fitzgerald said. "That stuff'll kill you."

"What about all the supplements you down during football—you're like a walking freakin' health store," Jomo joked as he pushed away his empty chili bowl and peeled open a banana.

"That's different," Fitzgerald said. "They've been checked out by coaches. Plus I'm using what's on approved lists for the pros. You want to be the best, then you follow the best."

Fitzie high-fived Jayson, although Jomo knew Jayson didn't take anything more than vitamins.

"I guess so," Jomo said. He chomped into his banana, then added, "Oh, yeah, I've been meaning to get you back that Ventilators disc." He took another bite, then went on, "They sound a helluva lot like Green Day, but not really. You know what I mean?"

Before Fitzie could answer, Sherman stood up with his tray and motioned to Terry with his head to follow him.

"Jayson, my brother, I trust that I will see you at the Black

Student Union meeting after school?" Sherman asked.

"I'll be there," Jayson said, tapping his chest before raising a fist.

"And bring your dog along." Sherman sniffed. "Maybe he'll learn something other than how to fetch and beg and act white."

"Why did you have to go there?" Jayson started to say, but Jomo cut him off.

"Well, congratulations, Sherm, old boy, you finally cracked a joke," he said, standing up and sarcastically clapping. He caught the attention of some nearby tables. "You gonna be the very next king of comedy," he went on. "I mean, you live in a gated community, you drive to school in a Mini, and ain't yo daddy a federal judge? But you know how to throw down for the cause."

Jayson tugged on Jomo's shirt hard enough to pull him down into his seat.

"One day, bitch," Sherman said, backing up a few steps, his finger aimed at Jomo. Jomo held his stare until Sherman abruptly turned and headed for the door.

"Okay, that was intense," Fitzie said nervously.

"No biggie." Jomo shrugged.

"Bullshit," Jayson said. "Jomo, don't go too far with Sherman. He's ain't big, but most of the brothers like him, and you don't need an enemy."

"Screw him," Jomo said, chomping another bite of the banana.

"I gotta bail," Fitzgerald said. "I'll catch you guys later. You going to be at the intrasquad meet tonight?"

"I'm going to try, yo," Jayson said, knuckle bumping him. "Be the man tonight, Fitzie."

"Yeah, good luck, dude," Jomo chimed in. He peeled his banana the rest of the way down and looked at his hands, his light-brown hands. His gnawed fingernails. He heard his mother in his head telling him that this too shall pass. Then he heard Sherman's voice telling him last year that he wasn't about shit, an uppity, high-yellow motherfudger who thinks he's better than everybody else. Jayson broke the silence.

"I know you're thinking about Sherman—"

"Pffft," Jomo scoffed. "That fraud is the last thing on my mind."

"Okay, Braveheart," Jayson said, leaning in. "I've known you for a long time, Jomo, a'ight? Don't pay him any mind. You're my dog, right? I got your back."

Jomo smiled.

"You're my brother," Jayson finished. "Until the end."

"It's Old School Saturday, and you've got the Wee Jock on Hot 95 FM."

Jomo rolled over, but the covers blocked his view, so he could make out only the bright red lines and curves of the tops of numbers of his alarm clock. He reached over to lift the clock and quickly realized that he wouldn't be seizing the day.

"Hot 95 time is—"

"Nine fifteen!" Jomo groaned. He'd mis-set the alarm the night before.

"Dammit, dammit, DAMMIT!" He slammed off the radio, then jumped out of bed and looked for shorts and a T-shirt.

It was the first time he'd missed a workout since he'd had the talk with his coach. Despite that initial humiliating session with Jeri, he was surprised at how much he was getting into his off-season training, mixing cardio, running, lifting, and pool, as well as resistance training in the gym. He even entered the downtown Y's New Year's Day 5K. He was surprised as hell he was even thinking about it.

But waking up late today meant that his whole day would be off. He had chores around the house, including laundry and bathroom detail. Plus he'd gotten a job working Saturdays, alternate Sundays, and two afternoons a week at the W. E. B. Du Bois & Martin Luther King Jr. Boys & Girls Club. His uncle was the director, but he dogged Jomo like he did everyone else. Sleep was a commodity Jomo couldn't afford. He found a relatively clean T-shirt and pulled it on.

And then he remembered Miranda Robertson. Oh, Lord, yes, Miranda. He fell back on the bed for a moment, and he could feel his cheeks get warm. He could still smell that scent—Chanel, she told him—from the night before.

The night before. Yeah, he and Jayson had gone to a mammoth house party around the corner from Jomo's house. Ordinarily, Jomo wouldn't have gone—parties weren't his thing. For one, he was still working those half-step moves brothers were doing twenty years ago. He didn't want be the freak. But he'd heard Miranda Robertson was going to be there. He'd seen her around—at church, at least when Mom was home and she dragged the family to midnight Christmas Mass and Easter Sunday. He'd even sat next to her once, back in sixth grade, at a joint Boy Scouts/Girl Scouts CPR seminar. He shared a practice dummy with her and five other people.

Jomo planned to go just to steal glances of her and dream up ways of talking to her. But since Jayson hooked up with Miranda's friend J'Leesa almost as soon as they got there, Jomo got to stand and fumble his words and thoughts with Miranda as J'Leesa and Jayson tore it up on the dance floor.

"So you go to Cathedral?" Jomo asked. He held a can of Coke so tight that the sides were denting.

"Yep," she said, nodding her head. Her brown eyes were impossibly sultry and sweet at the same time, and slight dimples formed around the corners of her lips as she smiled. She tilted her head like a curious cat sizing up some shiny oddity.

"That's cool," he said, jamming a free hand into his jeans pocket. He leaned against a door frame. He couldn't be sure if she was smiling out of interest or pity. He took his hand back out of his pocket. Then he began to think that she would think that he was some nervy freak with ADHD. *Chill, fool!* He forced himself to keep eye contact. To look lower would invite a serious rebuke.

She could've been giving him the right answers to every test he would take in high school, and still all he could do was focus on the silky black hair that cascaded down to her shoulders. It framed a beautiful cocoa-colored face, highlighted by her full, glossy lips. Her eyebrows were slender arches over her almond-shaped eyes. Yet there was so much more to her that had him mesmerized, like the way she gracefully walked while other people seemed to clump along. It was a female swagger—sexy, tough, but not bitchy. She was so cool that she made everything she did look effortless.

She was so cool, all he could think of was not saying something stupid, which made it impossible to say anything. The bass-heavy hip-hop beat rattled throughout the expansive manse, and thankfully Jomo noticed that it had shifted to a song he knew and liked.

"I like this one," he said.

"What?"

He moved in toward her left ear. "I like this song." He caught a whiff of her perfume, wanting to say something brilliant. Instead, he jerked backward, realizing he was dangerously close.

"Oh, yeah, Diddy's got it going on," she said, smiling and swaying to the music.

"It's the only song of his I like," he yelled. "Oh, I wanted to tell you that you smelled good."

Oh, my God. He felt like an even bigger idiot when Miranda looked at him and said nothing in reply.

As if by divine intervention, he caught himself about the sneeze. Desperate, he tried to stop.

"Hold on," he said, and ran to the bathroom.

He sneezed. It was loud. It was mucus laden. It would've been absolutely foul if he had done this in front of her. He washed his hands; the water splashed out of the bowl and onto his jeans.

"I can't fucking believe this," he growled.

Unable to find a towel, he wiped his hands on the sides of his blue oxford shirt. It didn't matter now.

Jomo walked out of the bathroom, and to his shock, Miranda was still standing there. Even more shocking, she looked like she was glad to see him.

"It's Chanel," she said, leaning toward him. "I'm glad you like it."

She leaned back, took a sip of a cherry Pepsi, and looked him up and down.

"Looks like you didn't make it in time, champ," she said, laughing.

"Hunh?" he said, before realizing that she meant the wet spots on his jeans. He loosened up.

"I'm sure you're stunned by my debonair nature, but this here," he said, waving his hand from head to toe, "this is typical me."

"Typical you?" she asked.

"Yeah," he said, and suddenly, maybe because she'd waited for him, he felt as if he could say anything. "You know how some guys are too tragically hip for the world? Well, I'm like the opposite of that. Part of my programming is to make Jayson look that much better."

"Programming." She laughed. "I'm not so sure about that."

As they talked, Jomo was surprised to find out that she knew of him. She remembered the CPR training, and she knew he played football. Her cousin was a running back at

Cathedral, and Jomo had had the misfortune of being plowed over by him last season. Jomo reminded her that he had also tackled her cousin a few times in the game, even popping the ball loose for a fumble.

By ten p.m. he'd impressed her enough with his ability to speak coherently about—and listen carefully to her opinions on—everything from movies and music to politics and J'Leesa's twisted sense of fashion that the party seemed to fade into the background. At midnight Jomo escorted Miranda home with her phone number stored in his cell phone and his number keyed into hers. Then, as he floated the six blocks from Miranda's place to his house, she called. Had something happened? Was she in trouble? Had he kept her out too late?

"Is everything okay?" Jomo asked, ready to run back six blocks.

"You know," she said, "I just called to make sure you got home safely." And they were still talking when his battery died three hours later, while he was sitting on his back porch, the cold not even bothering him.

Now, as Jomo jammed clothes into the hamper to take down to the washer, he realized the combination of sleep deprivation and the intoxicating effects of being in the presence of Miranda Robertson had clearly made him goof up setting the alarm clock.

He took the steps two at a time, plotting how to make up the time he'd already lost this morning. Instead of making an omelet, he could down a fruit smoothie; then he could still get in a quick run before he had to help his dad pound down some loose nails on the back porch. *Dad*, he groaned as he reached the landing. Coming up in a very special episode of *Jomo*: Heavy-Handed Responsibility Lecture, take Ten Thousand.

"Jomo," Edward Rodgers said as his son skittered into the kitchen. Jomo couldn't tell by the inflection if his father was annoyed.

"Before you start, Dad, I set the clock wrong," Jomo apologized.

He scrambled around the kitchen, pulling out his strawberry-flavored protein shake mix, skim milk, and a blender. That had been his breakfast for the past month, since the beginning of weight training.

"Jomo—"

"I know . . . I know, I'm late," Jomo said. He dumped the ingredients into the blender and turned it on.

"Jomo—"

"I'm just . . . quick run . . . I'll be ready to work . . . porch" is all that could be heard over the blender.

"Jomo—"

His dad got up.

"Like I said, my radio—"

"Boy!" His father turned off the blender. "Will you hush a minute? Come sit down."

Jomo froze. Something big was clearly coming down—bigger than his waking up late. He wondered if this was it—

his parents were finally getting a divorce. His body went to jelly. He left the drink in the blender and sat down. And was shocked when his father slammed down the sports section of the *Journal Ledger*, pointing to a story circled in red. The headline read:

FIVE TO WATCH NEXT YEAR.

It was the paper's annual all-metro-team edition. The all-metro first and second teams were made up of players from forty-five schools covering a twelve-county area. The five to watch were players who showed promise. With mouth agape, Jomo stared at a crisp color photograph of himself making a sweet one-handed interception against Claremont. *Holy shit!* Then he started reading.

Name: Jomo Andrew Rodgers
School: The Cranmer School
Position: Safety
Height: 5' 8"
Weight: 150

Although not big in stature, Jomo Rodgers can ball hawk with the best defensive backs in the state. He finished the season with 46 solo tackles and two interceptions.

Rodgers has speed, stamina, good coverage awareness, and decent hands. While he may be able to handle high school players, the big knock on him playing prime-time college football is his lack of size. If he were a couple of inches taller and 30 pounds heavier, Rodgers would be a recruiter's dream. Rodgers is one of ten returning defensive starters, giving Cranmer a legitimate shot at a state title.

Jomo looked up and saw his dad smiling.

"Congratulations," he said, throwing his hand up at Jomo for a high five. The smack of sound reverberated off the kitchen's white tiled walls and blond ash cabinets.

"Jayson called this morning while you were asleep. He tried to call your cell," his dad said. Jomo remembered it had gone dead the night before. "He wanted to congratulate you," his father said. "That and gloat about making the first team, as a sophomore."

"Jesus, seriously?" Jomo nearly screamed. "Whoa."

He skimmed the pages. Besides Jayson, the only other Cranmer player to be mentioned was Reardon, who was also selected to be on the first team, second year in a row.

"First team—oh my God," Jomo said, focusing on the write-up on Jayson.

"There isn't enough we can say about Jayson Caldwell," the

story began. Breathless highlights included "Cranmer's best player in a generation," "a major-college star in the making," and "probable—if he stays healthy—pro football prospect."

As far as write-ups go, that was the bomb. He imagined Jayson straining not to do the happy dance. Praise from the seniors, love, or something like it, from McPherson, now this—Jayson's swagger would only grow. Jomo imagined Jayson's mom not being able to contain her excitement. She was probably calling everybody she knew and would tell people in public who her boy was. He glanced at the clock. It was too early on the west coast to call his own mom. Early morning calls gave her heart attacks. He'd call her later, but it wouldn't be the same.

And yet he couldn't stop himself from going back over the phrase "the big knock on him." It always came down to his size. And then there was that damn "If He Was Just a Little Bit Taller . . ." award. Jayson got "Playing on Any Given Sunday." *He* got dissed. Couple of inches and thirty pounds. That's all he needed. He'd have instant swagger. He wouldn't have to be a smartass; he'd just look like he wasn't to be trifled with. If he were big like Jayson, there would be no "if only" or "the big knock on him." He started to read the article a third time when his father said, "While you were in your gentle slumber, dreaming of sugarplums or voluptuous women, or voluptuous women feeding you sugarplums, or whatever you dream about, I fixed the porch."

"Cool. Thanks, Dad. Can I—"

"Yes, take a long run. Go to the gym, whatever." His father blew on his coffee to cool it. "You deserve it. I'm proud of you."

Jomo's eyebrows arched, and his mouth went open for the second time that morning.

"But I thought you didn't like football anymore."

"Yeah, well." His dad shrugged. "You like it, so, well, there it is."

He brought his coffee cup up to his lips, and Jomo noticed his hand shaking. There had been a faculty get-together the night before, with drinks, of course; his father had probably gone out with Uncle Will for a beer or three afterward. Jomo also noticed that the ten-cup coffeepot was full: a French roast that when brewed right overwhelmed the kitchen. His parents loved the stuff so much that they had a special blend sent from a Minneapolis roaster, and it brought back memories of Saturday mornings of pancakes and eggs and bad jokes and laughter.

"Did we have just a wee too much to drink last night?" Jomo hinted.

"I'm fine, but you know how it is: yeah, yeah, kiss ass, blah, blah, grant, publish, me, me, me." His father drained the cup and poured himself some more coffee. "That reminds me, I ran into Del Fosse last night."

"Oh yeah?" Jomo folded his arms across his chest. No good could come from an impromptu parent-teacher meeting, particularly since he thought Fosse expected more out of him than any other kid in his U.S. history from 1946 to the present class.

"Yep. And she was very enthusiastic about your paper on the Freedom Riders." He then launched into an imitation of Jomo's haughty teacher. "Oh, Dr. Rodgers, you must be so pleased with his complete grasp of the subject matter. Clearly Jomo is taking after his father."

"Yeah, well." Jomo said, tensing up. Why was Dad mimicking his history teacher so sarcastically?

"Well?" His father stared at him. "*Well*, I looked like a fool for not having the faintest idea what she was talking about. It's not that I don't trust your academic skills, nor am I that amazed at your academic achievement. However, I do teach African American studies, and I would have thought you would have at least asked me a few questions, or at the very least told me when you were writing something in my area of expertise."

"I don't see what the big deal is." Jomo pushed away from the table, chair legs screeching across the floor tiles.

"I looked pretty clueless last night."

Jomo looked at his father in disbelief. It was amazing, truly amazing, how quickly his father could turn triumph into tragedy. It had been like this since Mom had left.

"Dad, why can't you just be happy?" Jomo fought to keep his tone from crossing the line. "I mean, she was complimenting you on my work. Generally parents are thrilled with that kind of news."

"I *am* happy," his father said, in a voice that didn't sound happy at all. "I just want to know why you chose not to tell me you were writing a paper on the Freedom Riders. I know the history—"

"By heart," Jomo snapped. "I know. I know you know the civil rights movement, the ins and outs and the wherefores and whys. And that's the problem. If I had gone to you, you would've done what you've always done when it comes to my history papers. You take over."

"And have you ever received a poor grade on a paper I helped with?" Edward asked.

"No, but—"

"In fact, have you ever gotten anything below an A?" Edward snapped.

"No, but—"

"My classes close fast during registration because I'm good, no, dammit, I am extraordinary at what I do. So what's the problem? You can't come to me?"

"No," Jomo said defiantly. As he struggled to find words, his eyes settled on the photograph on the refrigerator—Jomo and his parents at Jekyll Island in southern Georgia. His father had his arms around their shoulders. It was the summer before eighth grade. His dad had been invited to a conference and turned it into a vacation. They *were* close then—well, at least his father was less temperamental. *That* he knew. A burning sensation surged through him. This is what he got for choosing to stay with his father. Except that was bullshit. He chose his dad because even if his father would never admit it, he'd fall apart if he were left alone. And now Jomo had to deal with this horseshit.

Don't take it out on me because she left you and your obsessive bullshit! She loved you, but you couldn't take a sabbatical to allow her some glory. I should've left you here by yourself. That's what Jomo wanted to say. Instead, he turned on his heel and quickly walked toward the foyer, where his cross-trainers were.

"Obviously, there is a problem here," his dad called after him.

"Look, you're right and I'm wrong," Jomo said acerbically. "I should've crawled to you like a good son. Now may I go?"

"Do not get sarcastic with me, boy."

Jomo paused. He was on thin ice. It wasn't as though his father was going to slap him. He hadn't been spanked since he was a child. Spankings gave way to the more fashionable timeout. Then his punishments followed an escalating scale beginning with "Get out of my sight," then "Go to your room and contemplate why you are there," followed by "You are grounded" and culminating in "Your ass is *so* grounded."

He took a deep breath and in a strained voice said, "I'm sorry. All right?" It was the most bullshit apology he could muster. He added, for effect, "I just wanted to do the paper on my own. And I don't know why you can't deal with that."

"Fine," his father said. Jomo felt his father's stare but refused to look up. He double-knotted his left sneaker, then breezed past his father and out the door.

"Jomo!" his father said in a half yell, half yelp.

Jomo stopped but didn't turn around. He bounced lightly on his toes, braced for whatever was going to come next.

"I—"

"I know," Jomo said.

"Yeah." Edward sighed. "I'll see you when you get back."

Jomo trotted off without another word.

"So then he's like, 'Do not get sarcastic with me,' in that James Earl Jones voice of his," Jomo fumed as he pumped air into a misshapen basketball. His voice echoed in the empty gym of the Du Bois & King Boys & Girls Club. "Uncle Will, I just don't get him." He pulled the needle out of the ball, then spun the ball on the tip of his index finger. "And I don't think he wants to get me," Jomo continued. "Sometimes I don't think he even likes me."

Jomo's uncle, a taller, wider version of his dad, looked up from the knee brace he was adjusting and slapped Jomo's thigh.

"Hey now, li'l brother," he said, giving the brace one last tug. "I know your daddy can be, let's say stiff, rigid, tight, stoic, and any other adjective you want to use to describe his personality. He's been like that since we were kids. But he loves you, and you can't believe anything but that truth."

Jomo gave the ball a squeeze, then bounced it on the scuffed parquet floor. The lights were off, but sunlight bathed the gym. He passed the ball to his uncle.

"Oh, you wanna play, huh?" His uncle laughed, pulling on his goggles.

"You've got two knee braces and prescription goggles, old man." Jomo laughed too. "I think I can school you."

"Oh, you got your narrow ass in the paper and it's gone to your head," Will said as he dribbled toward the top of the key. "I remember when children respected their elders. I remember when shorties were *scared* of their elders."

Jomo crouched down into a defensive posture with his arms waist high. His uncle dribbled the ball slow and low to the floor.

"Court's in session," Will said in a pitch-perfect West Indian accent. "The honorable Judge Dread presiding."

Jomo knew Will was taunting him, begging him to dive in while he goofed. They'd both played enough chess to know not to play the easy opening move.

Will head faked to the right. Jomo didn't bite and kept up with his uncle's drive toward the left. Will pulled up for a ten-foot jumper with the fingertips of Jomo's hand in his face.

Swish.

"I can still hit the jumper like James Worthy, bad knee and all, baby," Will quipped.

"James who?"

"James who?" Will shouted, looking toward heaven. He jogged back to the top of the key. "Big Game James, boy, that's who! Lord, forgive the boy's ignorance. But is that not why you gave them ESPN Classic?"

The two played for a half hour, at first keeping score, but

eventually it didn't matter. Jomo loved this, grinding it out with his uncle.

Finally, dripping with sweat, they called it a game. They plopped down on a bench, resting back against the wall. Will sucked down water from a plain white plastic water bottle as Jomo opened an expensive energy drink.

"You know how much I paid for this water?" Will said, catching his breath. "Zip. Pure tap."

He took another swig.

"That crap doesn't do anything," he added, pointing at Jomo's aggressively stylized plastic bottle.

"Hey, it's got electrolytes and—"

"Yeah, and I'm sure the cat who ran from Marathon to Athens wouldn't have dropped dead if he'd filled up on electrolytes."

Jomo shook his head. "You had to reach way, way, way back to find that." He laughed.

"Six years of college, baby," Will said, pointing toward his head. "Now, your pops did it in three and a half years—he could've done it in three, if he hadn't played football his first two years."

Jomo pulled a towel out his gym bag and wiped sweat off his neck.

"Yeah, Dad was disciplined back then," he agreed. "You and Grandpa said he was a great athlete. So what happened? Why does he hate sports so much?"

"Your dad?" Will asked. "He doesn't hate sports. I mean,

come on, we still play racquetball here and there."

"What, like two or three times a year?" Jomo said. "And he doesn't even watch games on TV. He sometimes comes to my games, but even when he's there, he's really someplace else. Dag, I saw him grading papers at one game."

Will leaned forward.

"When we were kids, your dad was a lot like you, smart and a pretty good baller," Will said. "In the summer, you know, we used to play nonstop rounds of basketball, followed by baseball, followed by football. He was like a nerdy jock."

"So what happened?" Jomo downed the last bit of liquid from the bottle.

"Well." Will paused, running his hands back and forth over his closely shaven scalp. "College," he said finally, reaching into his gym bag and pulling out an aspirin bottle. "It got serious, and he felt that most big schools didn't give a damn about their athletes, particularly the ones who were poor and black and recruited to be athletes and not scholars. And he basically feels the same way now.

"It's why he stopped playing football after his sophomore year," he continued. "He got sick of being told that he was at school to play ball, not picket against South African apartheid or demonstrate about working conditions for janitors or start the Black Student Union." He laughed softly. "God bless him, your daddy thought it was his duty to right every wrong he saw."

"And what did you think?" Jomo asked. "You were

there—why didn't you go along? Or did you think Dad was wrong?"

"Nah, Ed was on a righteous mission," said Will. "I was in the Black Student Union, too, and I did a sit-in once with your father—he was in grad school at that point—against some such mess I don't remember. South Africa, Nicaragua, or something. Anyway, he got mad when I broke loose and went to football practice. We had separate goals, you know. He played football because he liked it, but his heart wasn't all the way there. I played football because it was the only thing I really loved. Don't get me wrong—I had good grades and I got my social work degree eventually. Damn, boy, this is ancient history."

He took a swig of water and rubbed the five-inch scar tissue that creased straight down his left knee. Just looking at it made Jomo's skin crawl.

"You really wanna know why your father is down on big-time sports?" Will asked.

Jomo nodded.

"Me."

"Because you didn't make it to the pros?" Jomo asked. "Because of your knee?"

"Yeah, but there's more, stuff we haven't talked about because" . . . He paused, and Jomo wondered if he would continue. But then his uncle drew a deep breath and said, "Well, you know, even after twenty something years, the hurt is still fresh, Jomo. I was a helluva good tailback. I tweaked my knee in my junior year, right before we got into our conference schedule. Nothing serious-serious, you know what I mean? But the football team was bustin' big. We'd even got some play in *Sports Illustrated*, and folks were saying that I was good to go as a third rounder, maybe even into the second round. The show went on without me, and I rehabbed as fast and hard as I could. Even though we were in a small conference, we got invited to the Tangerine Bowl against Tennessee. I was determined to play. And the coach didn't stop me. I had a good game, but my knee was killing me. Then I blew it out for real on some dinky sweep at the end of the game, when we were down by twenty-one. The game was over, and I should've been out. But Coach wanted us to play to the end."

Will paused again. He shook out two aspirin, downed them with a gulp of water, and then, to Jomo's surprise, pelted the aspirin bottle across the court. "I shouldn't have been on the field. Even with a medical redshirt, I was never any good again. They yanked my scholarship at the end of my junior year."

"Damn, that is whacked," Jomo said.

"Well, you know your father—he went absolutely buck wild. He blamed the coach . . . no, he threatened to *sue* him, because Coach had gone out and found a *team* doctor who said I was game ready. I never said a word, not even to your father, even though I knew deep down inside that the knee was still shaky."

"Yeah."

"As mad as he was at them, it felt like he was ten times as mad at me," Will said, standing up. "He said I had a slave mentality, I'd wrecked a possible pro career because I wanted to please my masters." He frowned at Jomo. "I played because I wanted to." His voice sounded more sad than angry. "But he wouldn't hear it. We were ready to throw down—two brothers ready to rumble, you know. I poked him in the chest. It was ugly. Your mother separated us. She tried to play peacemaker as best she could, but we were too damn pigheaded. Here we were at the same school and we might as well have been on opposite sides of the world. We basically communicated through your mom; your grandparents, too, when they were alive.

"Here's the deal, Jomo." His uncle sat back down and put his arm around Jomo's shoulders. "I could speak up for myself and I accepted the consequences; but your father—you know what he's like when he thinks somebody he loves has been wronged or when he thinks someone he loves is about to do wrong. He ain't never, ever going to change."

Jomo could identify with that. He decided not to press his uncle further, and for a moment they just sat and rested. Work ended the silence.

"C'mon, boy, we've wasted enough time," his uncle said, looking at a wall clock. "Your star may be on the rise, but I'm signing your paycheck, so back to work."

Jomo sprang up from the bench and dribbled toward the top of the free throw arch.

"Three, two, one," he yelled, then threw up a shot.

Clang! The ball slammed off the back of the rim and arched backward. Jomo turned toward his uncle, who burst out in laughter.

"Damn, those are some seriously sad ball skills," Will said, "Well, at least you've got football to fall back on."

Jomo and Jayson sat cross-legged on the bed in Jayson's cramped room and watched highlights of early-season college football games as well as the annual Army-Navy football game on SportsCenter.

"Second quarter, Army, down by ten after an interception, would get back into the game with a sixty-yard strike from Truzsinski to Maxwell," the studio host said as the replay was shown. "A four-and-out for the midshipmen, and the greatest Army duo since Grant and Sherman, since Bradley and Patton, team up again, this time for a seventy-two-yard touchdown play. . . ."

"Dude, would you go to West Point—or any of the academies?" Jomo suddenly asked.

Jayson hopped up and reached over to a small beige metal cabinet. He flipped through several file folders, pulled out two envelopes, and tossed them to Jomo. They were introductory letters from Annapolis and the Air Force Academy.

"Nah," Jayson said. "Too harsh, man. I read about the first year at these places—folks hollering and shouting, getting up at the break of dawn, and then you've got to give up four or five years after graduation. I'm down with the military, but I'm looking at the NFL, not getting shot at."

Jomo folded the Air Force Academy letter into a sleek paper airplane and sailed it out the door and into the hall. Jayson lived in a two-bedroom apartment that he shared with his mom and his cousin Mae, who was three years older than him. The wall-to-wall carpeting was old, as was the linoleum on kitchen and bathroom floors. The halls were lined with pictures of Jayson from the time of his birth to the present. The living room was sparely furnished, containing a twenty-year-old couch-loveseat-recliner set, a twenty-four-inch color TV, and a large glass case that held Jayson's trophies, jerseys, memento footballs, and news clippings. It was an intense shrine, but Jomo never thought of it as creepy. Indeed, this was a testament to Ms. Caldwell's cautious direction of her only child's development from, as she liked to say, "getting out of the ghetto and into the get more." And there was no doubt in Jomo's mind that his friend was going to get more.

"So how many letters have you gotten so far?" Jomo asked, leaning over into the cabinet. He saw catalogs and brochures from lots of schools he'd heard of, including fat ones from the Big 10, SEC, and Big 12. Purdue, Indiana, Notre Dame—the home-state teams—were in the mix.

"I don't know," Jayson said, now thumbing through shirts in his closet. "Maybe fifty or so. That includes a couple of IAA schools, too."

"Fifty," Jomo said. "Dah-yam."

"Yo, when is Miranda supposed to call?" Jayson said. "I'm hungry and I'm ready to roll."

Jomo looked at his watch. It was five fifteen.

"She's supposed to call about—"

Jomo had what had to be the most geeky and obnoxious ring tone ever—the old *Star Trek* theme. And at that moment the theme filled the room. Just to drive Jayson crazy, Jomo flipped the phone open like a communicator.

"Hey, we were just talking about you!" Jomo said into the receiver, trying to contain his giddiness. "No, no, nothing bad. Jayson's hungry and he wants to know when and where we are supposed to meet you and J'Leesa. . . . Yeah."

Jayson slipped on a starched white shirt and motioned to Jomo about its worthiness. Jomo gave a head nod and a thumbs-up.

"Okay, the food court at six, and then we'll go over to the theater." He laughed. "Yeah, we'll be home before ten. I promise. Cool. . . . Yeah, last night was fun—real fun. . . ."

His smile grew broader. He knew for sure his cheeks were getting red. Jayson was going to bust on him for that. And sure enough, Jomo looked up and saw him trying to contain his laughter. Jomo flipped him off, turned his back, and cupped the phone.

"I've never felt this way about anybody either," he said to Miranda. "I can't wait to see you. Bye. . . . No, you hang up first. Okay, on three. One. Two. No, we'll start now. One. Two. Three. Bye."

He closed the phone and turned to Jayson, who was nearly in tears.

"Oh my God, what's up with that?" Jayson asked, laughing even harder.

"What?" Jomo said, fumbling to slide the phone into his pocket.

"'No, you hang up. Okay, let's count,'" Jayson said in a sweetie-sweet voice. "You've known her for what, twenty-four hours . . ."

"Yes, but I feel like I've known her for at least forty-eight hours," Jomo quipped.

"You've gone all off the deep end," Jayson said, pushing Jomo. "You don't date enough. When's the last time you had an actual date?"

"I date . . . enough," Jomo said, balling up one of Jayson's clean sweat socks.

"Hooking up at a party don't cut."

"Fine, but I *have* dated."

"Past tense," Jayson hooted. "Okay, your last actual, for-real, go-hang-out-at-the-mall or go-to-the-movies date."

"Last summer, Amy Eckhert," Jomo said triumphantly.

Jayson nodded. "Yeah, and her parents were none too happy when they realized who was sniffing around their lily-white sweetness."

Jomo threw the sock at Jayson, then pulled out some gum. He offered Jayson a piece.

"Now you're hooking up with a sister from the block,"

Jayson continued, folding the stick in half before putting it in his mouth. "You've got to have a better rap. Make her come to you."

"Yeah, right. I forgot I was hanging with the great Jayson Caldwell, mac daddy Player number one. O great and wise one, how should I handle my business?"

"Negro, please," Jayson said as he brushed his hair. "Watch and learn, kid. Watch me, and see how a playa runs the game. Watch me. . . ."

"And see how J'Leesa puts you in your place, fool."

Jayson laughed.

"True that."

"I don't believe you," Miranda said with a big smile. She pointed a perfectly tapered finger at Jayson. "You've never cheated at anything?"

"Tests?" Jayson asked, chomping on a French fry. His arm was around J'Leesa, who pressed against him in the booth. "Nope."

"Homework?"

"Nah."

"Did only eight reps with weights when you were supposed to do ten or twelve?"

"No," he said, laughing. "As God as my witness—"

"Oh, you know he's on the straight and narrow, because he's evoked God," Jomo said.

"If I'm lying, I'm dying—I've never cheated on anything."

Miranda sat back, arms folded. She looked first at Jayson, then at J'Leesa.

"You better stick with him, girleen," she said. "This one pretends to be a player, but he just may be one of the few trustworthy brothers in the world."

"Ahem." Jomo cleared his throat. "And I am what?"

Miranda looked at him directly in the eye.

"You I don't know about," she said. "You drop catch phrases and have that look-at-me-I'm-not-like-the-rest-of-you snarkiness. You love the sound of your voice, even when it's just you in your head. You're different, but you really, really want to be bad-boy different."

Jomo, Jayson, and J'Leesa all laughed.

"What, you mean R. Kelly different?" Jomo said.

"No, not nasty." She laughed. "But you'd like to have thug appeal. You'd like to be the kind of brother who walks into a room and goes all Samuel Jackson at the first sign of trouble. But that's not you. Right now you've got a black version of *Friends* thing working." Then, as if reading his mind, she added, "Lucky for you I go for those guys."

"Yes, lucky me," said Jomo, his ego somewhat deflated. He was the black Chandler. Then he thought how pathetic it was that he even knew there was a character named Chandler to be black about.

"My boy's trying to get big, though," Jayson said. "He's training, hitting the weights. What are you benching right now?"

Jomo looked at Miranda and with great exaggeration puffed out his chest.

"I can't lift the stack, but I'm getting close," he assured her, flexing his arms.

"I know that's right," Jayson agreed, offering Jomo a high five.

"For football?" Miranda asked.

"Hunh?" Jomo answered.

"You're getting big solely for football?" she clarified.

"Yeah," Jomo and Jayson answered in unison.

"Because being big means being better," Miranda said.

"Not necessarily," Jomo countered.

"Fine, but being small or out of shape doesn't help, right?" Jomo and Jayson nodded.

"Okay, so let me ask you a question," Miranda said, pursing her lips.

"Oh, she's going Oprah now," J'Leesa warned.

"If you could get away with taking steroids, would you do it?"

"Hell no," Jayson responded first, vigorously shaking his head. "Like I said, I don't cheat, but even besides that, you know what the stuff does to your body beyond getting ripped—"

"What if the drug had no side effects?" Miranda interrupted.

"Now you're just being silly." Jayson took his arm from around J'Leesa and leaned in toward Miranda. Debate on.

"Really now," she said. "Even if it meant the team would win more games and you'd get more play from, say, the pros."

"I don't cheat. For nobody," Jayson said, incensed. "I don't want to cheat, and I don't need to. I've got coaches dialing and texting me all the time."

"Interesting," Miranda said. "And you, Jomo?"

Jomo thought for a second, then stuck a French fry into his mouth. He knew they knew that he was feigning, but it was fun to pretend that he could be devious.

"J'Leesa, you're awfully quiet," he said.

"That's because you all talk more shit about stuff nobody cares about than I ever thought possible," she said, twirling the straw in her cup. She took a long sip, hitting the bottom of what was left in the cup. She shook the cup at Jayson.

"Baby, please."

"A'ight, Boo." Jayson grabbed the cup and headed for the soda fountain.

"Don't forget my lemon slice, baby," J'Leesa called out.

"Trained?" Miranda said.

"No, he's just like that," J'Leesa said. "Jomo is like that too. He's a good guy. A little goofy, but he's always had my Boo's back. Jomo was brought up right."

"So, you wouldn't shoot yourself in the ass to grow those pecs?" Miranda said, nudging Jomo.

His leg brushed up against Miranda's. He grabbed her hand under the table and noticed the surprised but happy look on her face.

"Do you ever get tired of talking?" he asked.

"Only when you get tired of listening," she said.

"Can y'all wannabes sound anymore pathetic?" J'Leesa groaned. "The two biggest big-headed folks I know have finally found each other."

Jomo surveyed the chessboard for what, at least based on his father's sighing and foot tapping, seemed an interminable amount of time. His impatience was as irritating to Jomo as the fact that he was winning despite two glasses of wine, and he was nursing a third.

"Are you going to make a move tonight?" his father grunted. "I've got papers to grade."

Jomo quickly moved his queen in a gambit that he thought would force his father to sacrifice his lone rook, offering the opening he needed to at least draw the game if not pull off a rare win. His dad took a long sip of his cabernet, set down the glass, then unexpectedly moved his knight into a space that appeared to be as wide open as prairie pasture.

"Check in three moves," he said cockily. "Mate in a few moves after that."

"Why do you do that?" Jomo said.

"Because eventually you'll learn not to let me get into your head," his father said, picking up his glass again. "Until then I'll enjoy rattling around up in there, making you rethink every move two, three, and four times."

He hovered over the board and then looked at Jomo.

"I'll show what's going to happen. . . ."

"Silence," Jomo yelped.

His father let out a sardonic, movie-quality laugh. Jomo was spared more of it because the phone rang. He let his father pick it up—all his friends called his cell.

"Hello?" his father said fluidly, then he paused. "That's Jomo, not Joe-Moe—it's all one word."

Jomo looked up from the chessboard.

"Who's calling?" his father continued. Another pause. "And you're from where, Mr. Fox?" Another pause. Jomo wondered who Mr. Fox was and why was he calling about him.

"Missouri A&M, yes, out near Kansas City, right?"

Holy crap, a football call, from a Division I school. A small one, but still a Division I program. Jomo dropped his rook and excitedly signaled to his father.

"Put him on speaker phone," he whispered. His father shook his head no, motioned Jomo to keep playing, and said into the phone, "Oh, really, you saw Jomo play against Madison County. . . . Yes, he and Jayson are like brothers." Jomo frowned—his moment in the sun had to include Jayson. Still, he silently pleaded with his father, who continued to ignore him. "No, Mr. Fox. . . . Okay, Coach Fox, I was in Chicago. . . . A black history conference. I'm a professor."

"Dad," Jomo said in a louder voice. "Speaker. Come on!" Jomo knocked his father's rook off the board for added affect. His father shot him a look, then stabbed at the speaker button on the phone.

"Well, Mr. Rodgers," the flat nasal voice sounding through the speaker. "I'm the defensive backs coach and recruiting coordinator for Missouri A&M, and—"

"Can you hold just a sec?" Jomo's dad said into the phone. "The end is coming soon," he told Jomo.

"Sir?" Fox said.

"Not you," his father said sternly. "What's this about again?"

"You sound like you're in an echo chamber."

"I had to put you on speaker phone," his father said. "I'm working."

"Okay, yes," Fox said. "Umm, well, we're interested in getting your son here. We'd like Jayson Caldwell, too. Those two together are quite a powerful pair."

Damn, Jomo thought, what was he, the backup date to the prom? They only wanted him if they got Jayson too.

Fox kept talking. "Mr. Rodgers, this is a fantastic school, with a fine tradition. Like you said, we're located right outside Kansas City—that's in the western part of the state—"

Jomo's father rolled his eyes. This Fox guy wasn't making

a good impression, Jomo decided, and wondered if he should take the phone before it got real bad. But his father was already interrupting the recruiter. "Yes, it's next to Kansas—a free state to Missouri's slave state," he told Fox in a voice so polite, it was condescending. *Aww damn, why?* Jomo could feel fury rising. First, it was his father's way of letting Fox know that he knew more than him. Second, Jomo just wanted his father to let the guy talk. Really, what he wanted was for Fox to talk to *him* about this possible opportunity.

He stared hard at the chessboard and saw an opening. He moved quickly, this time taking a pawn. His father smirked and immediately responded, taking out Jomo's bishop, which had been protecting his king.

"Check," he whispered.

"I see you're up on your geography and history, sir," Fox was saying, laughing. "Anyway, Mr. Rodgers, we are an up-and-coming program. Last year, we went seven and five, and we were invited to the Orchid Bowl down in Fort Lauderdale. It was the program's first bowl game since going Division I-A, I'm sorry, the Division I-Bowl Championship, in '98. With a generous donation from our boosters, we're in the process of upgrading our facilities, putting in field turf, a new weight room, new locker rooms—and installing a high-definition scoreboard. And Mr. Rodgers—can I call you Ed?"

"No."

"Sir?"

"No, I'd prefer that you not call me Ed," Jomo's father said, finishing off the last of the wine. "Hold on." He waved his empty glass at Jomo, who scrambled to the kitchen.

"Continue," he said.

"Er, yes," Fox spluttered. "The Mid-Continent Athletic Conference just signed a new contract to have the league's game of the week shown every Wednesday night on the new All College Sports Network. We're going to be on regional TV too. It'll be great exposure for your son to show off his talent."

Jomo hustled back in the room with the bottle and poured the last of it into his father's glass.

"His talent?" Edward said, swirling the wine in the glass before taking another swig.

Jomo sat as close to the phone as he dared. Then his own phone screeched out the opening notes of the *Star Trek* theme. Damn! He leaped back up and ran to the kitchen. It was Miranda.

"I've got to call you back—sorry," he said.

"Okay—"

Jomo snapped the phone shut and tiptoed back to the living room.

"And I've seen him on tape as well, and your son has got raw talent. A tremendous hitter for his size. We wish he was a little heavier, but we think we can work around that problem."

Great, his size again. But still, if it was that bad, they wouldn't have called, Jomo reasoned.

"He'd make a great writer, maybe a journalist," his father told Fox dismissively. Jomo glared at him.

"Sir?"

"Jomo. He's got a natural empathy that stops him from being a know-it-all jerk like me and pushes him to be like his mother. Inquisitive. Did the tape not show his inquisitiveness?"

"Excuse me, sir? I don't follow."

Now his father was buzzing toward drunkenness. Of all the times for this to happen, Goddammit! Maybe if he kicked the cord out of the wall, Jomo thought. Maybe the world could end. This was going to be a call that got talked about among recruiters—the drunken jackass father.

"Coach Fox. Can I call you Johnny?" Jomo's father didn't wait for answer. "All I've heard is football. I remember A&M had a great sociology department, all sorts of crazy hippies studying everything from youth violence to farm families. Goddamn, those folks were brilliant. But they closed the school. Too many radicals, I think. Do *you* think they had too many radicals?"

"Dad," Jomo whispered, more embarrassed for his father than himself at this point. "Dad, stop."

"Sir, I—I mean, I don't understand—," Fox said.

"Of course you don't. Never mind. I suspect you'd like to talk to Jomo. Jomo! A gentleman from the Show-Me State's agricultural and mechanical university would like to talk to you about playing football."

Well, thank God it wasn't USC or Ohio State. Jomo picked up the cordless receiver and took it off the speaker phone.

"Hello. This is Jomo," he said, walking away from his father and toward the staircase.

"Jomo," Fox said, his voice wary. "This is John Fox. I'm the defensive backs coach and recruiting coordinator at Missouri A&M—"

"I saw the Orchid Bowl—good comeback in the second half to get it to overtime," Jomo said, climbing up the steps to his room. "Sorry about the loss, though."

"You saw us, huh?" Fox said, his voice perking up. "Yeah, we gave 'em hell in the second half. To be honest, we just didn't have the talent to pull away from those guys. Some of my boys got red brained and couldn't hack the pressure. That's why I'm calling. I got some tape on you, tape of you playing in the Cathedral game." God. Jomo hoped it wasn't when he got run over by Cathedral's tight end. "Like I told your dad, I saw some raw talent. You're a little undersized," Fox was saying, "but you've got football smarts. Have you gotten any other calls?"

"Me? No," Jomo said. He slipped into his desk chair and began a Google search on the A&M football program. "You're my first. Hopefully not my only." *Oh, crap, that sounded stupid.* "What I meant—," Jomo said, trying to minimize the damage.

"It's okay, kid. I'm not going to be the only one to call you. First off, I'm only allowed to call you once this school year. So

I'm hoping I can make the right pitch to you now. But you can call me as much as you want. Let me tell you what I see in your future, and how A&M can help you get there."

The pitch went on for fifteen minutes, and Jomo was realizing that he was more flattered by the attention he was receiving from a Division I coach than impressed about playing football at a cow college in a small conference. When he finally got off the phone, he ran downstairs.

His father was curled on the couch. His wine glass had overturned. Splashes of red splotched some ungraded papers and books with multicolored sticky notes peeking out from between the pages. His father had finished the chess game: Jomo's king lay on its side. A DVD of family memories flickered on the TV, the montage of pictures and video his mother had put together as a wedding anniversary present a couple years back: the family at the beach, Jomo and his father playing chess, Jomo and his mother in the snow, Jomo's father dipping his mother and kissing her at their twentieth anniversary party—the last one before she'd left. The TV sound was down, but Billie Holiday was singing "God Bless the Child" on the stereo.

Jomo turned down the music and turned off the TV and DVD player. He gathered the papers and books together in a neater pile on the ottoman, then placed a quilt gently over his father, who stirred for a moment, before settling back to sleep. He turned off the light and walked upstairs, to study for his semester final in U.S. history from 1946—also known as

MoAm, for "modern American history." He tried to concentrate on the Cuban missile crisis, but all he could think about was the recruiting call. So what if it wasn't one of the big-time colleges that was calling Jayson? It was still pretty cool to be on somebody's list. He wondered if they'd give him a full ride or if this was a chance to walk on and then win a scholarship. Even so, there would be perks—being on television being the biggest. And girls, yes, college women, but he was still all about Miranda. His thoughts were interrupted by a ding from his computer. It was an instant message.

"Hello from Seattle."

It was his mom. Jomo smiled. His mom was so cool—she'd caught on to IMing a lot sooner than his friends' moms. And it was, sometimes, easier than talking, which they did about twice a week.

"Studying 4 history final."

"How's everything else?"

"I'm fine. Nothing to report."

"Your dad?"

Jomo stopped typing. He pursed his lips and quickly weighed between telling the truth and withholding the truth.

"Fine," he typed. "Got 2 go. Talk tomorrow?"

06

"Eleven!" Jomo huffed out then sucked in a huge gulp of air. His legs burned. His knees pushed back into his torso as far they could go without slamming the 150-pound stack of weights into the rest of the plates.

"One more," Jeri urged him. "One more, kid. Last set. Last set."

He gave one more push. "Twelve!" This time he let the stack drop, and the echo reverberated around the empty room. He pulled his legs from the metal plate but was too tired to get up. Jeri marked down that he'd done two sets of twelve repetitions on the leg press.

"Why do I . . . feel like my legs . . . are going to fall off?" Jomo panted. He swiped sweat off his forehead and wiped it on his shorts. Jeri smiled gently.

"I *know* you're excited about that A&M call, and you've shown improvement in all phases—"

"Improvement?" he interrupted. "It doesn't show. I've got to pack on the muscle if I want colleges to take me seriously."

Jeri sat down on the firm seat of the leg curl machine. "You—and not just you really, almost everybody on the team—you're too eager to see big muscles, washboard abs, and Lance Armstrong endurance. Look at the numbers, kid. You're on target. I promise, by training camp you'll be in shape for the season. And you'll need it, because I hear two-a-days are going to be a beast."

Jomo stood up but quickly dropped back down on the set cushion. His legs were still burning, though he had to admit they didn't sting quite as much as they had when he'd first started lifting a month ago. But it was taking *so* long. He chanced a question.

"I know you're down on powders and stuff—," Jomo said.

"I know where you're going with this," she cut him off.

"But what if—"

"No, Jomo. I can't tell you—"

"But some guys use them, and Coach has his approved list, and the guys say—"

"In my opinion you're better off—"

"—they get results."

Jeri stopped. She looked at Jomo for a moment.

"Jomo, look at the chart," she said softly but deliberately.

"You're on pace to be in far better shape than you were when you finished last season. There are no shortcuts."

"I know, I know," Jomo said. "But I'm looking at some of the guys who say they've been using supplements, and I've got to tell you, the results don't lie. I've got a chance to play D-I football. You don't know what that's like."

Jomo wanted an answer, but Jeri wasn't talking.

"Supplements?" he asked.

"Well, what happens if they don't help you to build as much and as fast as you want?" she asked. He noticed her tone was more philosophical. "Why not juicing?" she continued.

"I'm not saying that—"

"I know, but wouldn't that be the next logical step?" Jeri asked. "Steroids and human growth hormone—they produce muscle, but they also reduce muscle breakdown. These powders aren't as harsh, but it's a shortcut. The reason I suggested that you lift three, maybe four times a week, no more, is that your muscles need time to recover. Performance enhancers allow you to lift more often, building more muscle faster. But the side effects are devastating."

"I heard no one has ever died from steroids," Jomo argued.

"Even if that were the case," Jeri said, "there are proven side effects on young athletes."

"I know, mood swings, acne, blah blah," he said.

"Yeah, and enlarged heart muscles, liver tumors, impotence, and other nasty stuff," she added. "Like I said, if you do it the right way, you're going to be stronger—a lot stronger—

than you were at the end of last season. Yep, there are easier ways to get ripped, but this is the only safe way." Jeri looked at her watch. "All right, hit the showers, keep up the good work, and I'll see you in February."

"February?" Jomo asked in surprise.

"I'm going to be riding in a couple of pro-am mountain bike races on the West Coast. I'm trying to see if I've still got something left."

"You race mountain bikes?"

"Yep."

"Seriously. You?"

"Don't be so surprised," she said with a laugh. "I rode for a top cat 1 team, had major sponsorships. I even modeled for a cheesy bike-shop calendar—you know, looking all hard and cute. It was all good, until I fell off my bike and landed on my right knee. Just crushed it."

"So you got dropped?"

"No, I just stopped racing."

"But . . . but why?"

She paused, as if thinking something through. Then she said, "To be honest, I stopped because of the b.s. You know, here I was, twenty years old, in the best shape of my life, and my coach wants me to go to some doctor and get a B-twelve shot."

"So . . ."

"So, B-twelve shots are for elderly people. It doesn't give you any more energy. I knew what they wanted to do—have me take steroids and keep racing. And while drug testing is rare in high school, they do test in pro cycling, and if I got caught, that would be my butt."

"I think I would've gone along with the program." Jomo laughed. "People pass those tests all the time, right?"

Jeri slammed Jomo's folder down on the leg curl bench. The contents scattered around the machine. She squatted and started gathering the papers, then stopped and looked at Jomo, her eyes tightened into slits.

"I bailed," she said. "I was either too stupid or too stubborn, or maybe it was the voice of my old man in my head telling me that I had to do it the right way. No shortcuts. It's an easy choice until you have to make it. But lucky for me, my injury led me to you jackasses, who want everything right now," she growled.

"Jeri, I'm sorry. I didn't mean—"

"Yeah, whatever," she said. Jomo followed her to her makeshift desk, which was nothing more than a wooden door set atop two black metal filing cases. He didn't know what to say.

"No, really, I'm sorry," he said. He felt like a preschooler searching for the right tone of forgiveness for pushing his teacher's last button.

Jeri threw herself into the black faux-leather rolling chair and crammed Jomo's folder into a cabinet. She slammed the door shut. The bang echoed off the walls. Jomo froze. He didn't know whether to stay or flee. Jeri rubbed her eyes and sighed sleepily.

"I know what I'm talking about when it comes to this stuff," she said. "I know how it is. I get it. You want to be bigger now. But just stick to the plan."

She looked up at Jomo. "I've seen that stuff wreck a lot of careers," she said, her tone softer but her words sterner.

"*Look*, I'm not going to lie—I was tempted too," she continued. "Not just by steroids, but EPO and all the other stuff that was supposed to make me a better rider. I could've been on the podium much more than I was, but I didn't want to live that lie. You know what I mean?"

Jomo didn't know what to say.

"And cue music and fade to next scene," Jeri said to lighten the mood. "I know it sounds corny, but I could hear my dad in my head. Guilt—it sometimes does a body good."

Jomo laughed and felt the muscles in his neck loosen. "I feel you. And I am sorry. Sometimes my mouth runs and I don't think." Jomo paused. He couldn't tell if she was still upset. "Are we cool?" he asked.

"Yeah, we're cool," she said. "Well, I'm cool. You're kind of dippy with a smattering of cool."

"A'ight. Fair enough." He smiled. "Good luck. I'll see you in February."

Jomo headed through a long, well-lit corridor toward the locker rooms. This was Cranmer's de facto walk of fame: the trophies, the plaques dedicated to great players going way back to the beginning. There was the first picture of the first team— twelve players, one manager, and the school's founder, Colonel

Barnabas Chisholm. There was the 1916 photo of the school's first state championship team, which went undefeated. Their names were etched into the football. Cranmer's military past could also be found on the walls of the corridor. Chisholm's favorite saying, "Better to be bloodied on this football field than to be scared and lost on the battlefield," was set in calligraphy and gilt framed. This is what Chisholm told the mother of fifteen-year-old Wilbur "Pudgy" Myers after he broke his hand in a game in 1922. Myers served in World War II and went on to command a division in the Korean War before becoming a state senator and, later, lieutenant governor.

This was the lore that every Cranmer football player knew. At the start of every season each player on the freshman and varsity teams got a playbook and a team history, known as The Book. Studying the playbook was a given. Players were expected to memorize The Book. There was a written *test* on The Book. Coaches and upperclassmen, in a tradition going back to the days when the school was a military academy, hazed underclassmen by testing them on their knowledge of The Book. Failure required the offender to "Duck the Quad"— squat and waddle like a duck around the quad while reciting the following:

Quack, quack, I'm sorry I don't know a simple fact.
Quack, quack, I ought to get a kick in the back.
Quack, quack, thanks due to mercy and my own bad luck,
Quack, quack, I get to waddle like a duck.

People swore that was why Cranmer's footballers had huge thighs. Jomo looked at a black-and-white photo of military-uniformed boys in the 1950s Ducking the Quad, and he smiled. Ducking the Quad sucked big time. Every one of his teammates had Ducked the Quad at least once; Jomo was a repeat offender. Except for Jayson. He fell asleep reading The Book and studied it in the morning in the way some folks read the Bible.

Beside the photo was the one thing that Jomo paused at nearly every time he walked down the hall. It was the plaque dedicated to Benedict "Big Ben" Fizer. Fizer was a brainy-brawny brother from Detroit who attended Cranmer from 1959 to 1961. He was the first African American to graduate from the school; several had attended before but left because of the racism. Fizer's accomplishments as a two-way sports star were legendary: His single-season records for rushing and tackles stood for thirty years. It took two different guys to break them, because nobody played offense *and* defense anymore. But what most impressed Jomo and Jayson and nearly every other black kid who attended Cranmer was Fizer's resolve. As a freshman he was the only black student on campus, and other than the lunch ladies and the janitor, no one talked to him for the first nine months. He graduated number two in his class, and, as Jomo once heard from an alumnus who knew Fizer, "The man didn't take any shit off of any one of us." *You got to respect that*, Jomo had thought at the time.

Fitzer eventually earned a spot at West Point, was commissioned, and later died in Vietnam. He was one of two Cranmer grads to earn the Congressional Medal of Honor.

While Jomo stared at Fizer's picture, various conversations came back to him—with Jeri and his father and his uncle—about doing things the right way, taking responsibility, not taking the shortcut. Yeah. Yeah, but Jomo knew that size *did* matter. He knew he was smart and he could anticipate plays, but like he'd heard and read, you can't teach size. True, but he knew there were ways around that.

He thought about this more as he let the water in the shower pound off his head. Jomo knew what recruiters wanted: muscle, power, speed, football sense. Other than football sense, he lacked them all. He could have them though—with a little help. But how true was he being to his own beliefs if he was willing to sell his soul for a bought body? He was so into his own head that he nearly jumped out of his skin when he felt a sharp jab in his upper back.

"Shit!" Jomo whipped around, almost losing his balance. It was Trey using his fingers as a mock pistol.

"Oh my God, dude, I so had you," Trey said, laughing.

"Asshole," Jomo yelled. "Jesus!"

Trey turned on the shower across from Jomo.

"What are you so wrapped up about?" Trey shouted above the water, lathering up.

"Just thinking."

"Yeah, about what?"

Jomo shrugged.

"I know it's not Miranda." Trey laughed again. "I suspect Li'l Jomo would be at full attention."

"You're a sick little monkey," Jomo said, walking out of the shower. He grabbed his towel off the rack, dried off, then wrapped the towel around his midsection before pulling a toothbrush and toothpaste out of his kit.

Seeing his reflection in the mirror over the sink as he brushed didn't help his mood. He couldn't see a lick of difference from the weight training.

Trey sidled up next to him. Jomo spit out a mouthful of toothpaste. He looked over to see Trey swallow a handful of pills with a sip of Coke.

"What—"

Trey cut off Jomo. "Creatine, dude, you want some?"

"Creatine?"

"Yeah—helps keep the muscles up."

Keep the muscles up? What the hell? Jomo must have looked as confused as he felt, because Trey added, "Why in the hell do you think I'm able to lift every day without fucking myself up?"

"I didn't know . . . ," Jomo began, nervously. He looked furtively around the locker room and lowered his voice. "I mean, does anyone know?"

"My dad. He's the one who suggested it," Trey said, spreading toothpaste on his brush. "You can get it off the shelf at health stores."

Jomo did a double take. "Your dad . . . ?"

"Shit, Jomo, a lot of guys use stuff like this."

"Really? Like who?"

"Fitzie for one."

"Fitzie? Come on."

Trey laughed. "God, Fitzie's like a freaking pharmacist. How do you think he loses and gains weight so fast? That dude has hookups for everything and anything."

"Steriods?"

"Fitzie? Nah. Well, maybe not for himself."

"But I've never heard . . ."

"That's because you hang with Jayson. He's God blessed while the rest of us are Goddamned human."

As he walked to class, Jomo thought about what Trey had told him. If it was going on at Cranmer, it was going on at Cathedral and Madison County and every school they would play next year. And yeah, Trey was right: Jayson was gifted a DNA ladder that made him more talented than most people. And the fact that he worked harder than anyone else at playing football only made him that much better. Damn. He knew he needed to go from 150 to 180 at least, and a lot of it had to be muscle. He needed to go all out. As cool as Jeri was, he didn't see that happening with her plan. It was time to do some research.

Declan Aloysius Gardner was universally loved. He taught drama and speech and coached the debate team and the field events for track. His classes were tough, but he was tougher. His big booming voice matched his size—a six-foot, barrel-chested, somewhat jiggle-bellied man with a full beard. The kids called him Dec, but not to his face. That was a no-no Jomo committed early in his freshman year, in a hazing incident when a senior told him it was okay to call him that. The heat from the fiery stare he gave Jomo could've melted the polar ice caps. From then on it was "Mr. Gardner." Really, he liked Jomo; told him so at the end of his freshman year, when Jomo had had to perform with several other "volunteer" freshmen in an all-male version of the "I Hope I Get It" number from *A Chorus Line* in the school's follies and revue. Tradition was a big thing at Cranmer; you didn't have to like it, but you did have to smile and take it politely.

Jomo had an elective available in his sophomore year, so he took Gardner's speech class. The classroom was decorated by those deemed by Gardner to be great orators and dramatists: Sophocles, Shakespeare, Martin Luther King Jr., and even Ronald Reagan.

Jomo walked into his second class of the day, and saw Trey at the end of one of two long tables. There were only twenty students in the class. A large flat-panel TV was center front. Before Jomo could say anything to Trey, Gardner walked in. He tossed a heavy-looking black satchel onto the desk.

"Gentlemen," he said, taking off his blue blazer, "welcome to Speech I. Now take a look to the sides of you, to the front of you, and, finally, behind you. If your parents have paid tuition, most likely you'll be here at the end of the semester."

This drew a couple of chuckles.

"But more than anything else, you men of Cranmer, I expect you to leave this class knowing that giving a speech isn't about jokes, cards, and charts. It's about connecting with the audience," Gardner said.

He walked over to a picture of Reagan at the Berlin Wall. "Even if you didn't like his politics—and I didn't at the time"—he turned to arch an eyebrow at his students—"the man connected with people. It's why he was called the Great Communicator."

"So was Hitler," someone shouted out as a joke. Gardner didn't break.

"Don't be so cynical," he said. "Point not well taken, young Mr. Keefer, and I'll see you after class."

Damn, Jomo thought, *he knows voices and he doesn't take any crap.* Jomo was hooked.

"This class isn't about agreeing with the text," Gardner said. "I want you to leave here learning how to make a persuasive speech, one with heart and passion, not heat and blubber."

Jomo nodded; he was digging it.

"Anybody here ever seen or heard Martin Luther King's 'I have a dream' speech?" Jomo shot his hand up.

"Of course, Mr. Rodgers. Given who your father is, I expect you know the speech by heart," Gardner said. Jomo didn't, but he nodded anyway.

Gardner looked around at the other raised hands in the room. "Good. Most of you've heard of it. Okay, that's where we're going to start today. Why? Because it's a speech that changed this country. It connected in 1963 and it still does today. We're going to break it down for the next couple of classes. After that, we're going to roll back to Shakespeare and Marc Antony and talk about repetition. Repetition. Repetition."

Gardner stopped and looked at the class.

"Okay, stupid joke, but I will expect you philistines to laugh at good jokes when you hear them."

07

Jomo stood out near the dumpster of Brutus's Chicken Shack. It was cold, but not cold enough to mask the smell of rotting fried chicken and other waste that was making him nauseous. He walked around the dumpster, opened and closed his phone again and again.

"Don't be a wuss," he finally said out loud. This time he punched in numbers fast and deliberate. Before he could change his mind, he hit send, took a deep breath, and rocked back and forth on his heels.

"Yo, yo, Fitzie. It's me, Jomo." Jomo plugged his ears to drown out the noise from cars whizzing down the boulevard.

"Yeah, I'm outside, at Brutus's," Jomo said, shaking his head and laughing. "No, I'm not bringing you some biscuits.

"Shit yeah, it's freezing. Look, let me ask you a question . . .

No, it's not about sex. Why in the hell would I call *you* for advice?

"Puh-lease, fool. I've seen your little uncircumcised dick in the shower.

"I think the phrase is 'latent homosexual,' and no, I'm not. We're all naked in the shower. That shit is hard to miss.

"Fitzie, freeze. Look, man, here's the deal. Do you remember a couple of weeks ago you told me about the guys who were kicked off the team for doping?

"Yeah, okay, if—and this a hypothetical—if I was looking to, say, get bigger, you know, faster than I am in my current weight routine, do you know somebody who could hook me up?

"It's for a paper I'm doing for persuasive writing.

"Of course it's bullshit, but you asked and I didn't want to sound desperate.

"I'm not *saying* you do it, but Fitzie, I know you know who does, and I know you know somebody who can hook me up. All I'm asking is if you can set me on the correct path.

"Why do you think I'm thinking about it?

"Now you sound like a fucking guidance counselor.

"A brother can ask, can't he? All I'm asking is that you give me the name of someone who can answer my questions.

"Jesus Christ, Fitzie, you're not going to be implicated in anything.

"Well, do you use the shit?

"Do you sell the shit?

"Do you make money off of the shit?

"All right, then how are you going to get implicated in something that you're not involved in?

"What do you mean you don't know? I've heard that you know.

"Okay, then you think about it.

"Yeah, either call or text me.

"I'm not going to say anything to anybody, so don't worry about me.

"Okay, this is on the down low.

"Yes, on the way, way, way down low, Fitzie. I swear to God.

"No, that's going too far. Plus, how is swearing on a stack of Bibles any more of a symbol of my fidelity than just swearing to God on a freakin' telephone in front of a fast-food dumpster?

"Yeah, fidelity. Look it up. Loyalty. Faithfulness.

"Because I didn't want to use those words. Oh, for fuck sake, good-bye.

"Peace."

Part II

"THE ROAD TO EASY STREET GOES THROUGH THE SEWER."

—John Madden,
Hall of Fame coach, and broadcaster

"Is this Joe-Moe?" The voice was older, with an easy drawl that stretched out the syllables in his name.

"Yeah? Who is this?"

"It's your lucky day."

"Hunh?"

"Are you still looking to get big?"

Oh, shit, this is real, Jomo thought. His father was out with Uncle Will, he was alone in the house, yet he felt the need to drastically reduce the volume of his voice. He looked around, even though he was in his bedroom, and even went as far as to cup his hand around the mouthpiece.

"A . . . fr . . ."

"You're breaking up."

Jomo uncupped the mouthpiece.

"Are you a friend of Fitzie's?"

"Who the fuck is that?"

"Wha—"

"Are you fuckin' interested or what? I don't need this shit."

"I'm—I'm interested."

"All right, you got time to meet tomorrow?"

"I've got school—"

"School? For shit sake, how old are you? Goddamn. Never mind. Bring a hundred and fifty dollars. Cash. Just meet me at . . ."

Jomo wrote down the instructions and then clicked off the phone. He leaped from his chair and started pacing around his room. His heart raced, his brain raced. For all his wish to be a badass, Jomo knew he was, at least up to this point, more talker than doer. At this moment the reason became crystal clear: He was scared. It was fear; fear of being caught, fear of losing control.

His stomach was beginning to churn. What was he doing? It wasn't like he was going to score some crack, he reasoned, but still, where did performance-enhancing drugs come in to play? Illegal, sure, but they weren't like heroin, right? He paced faster. And the faster he paced, the more worked up he got.

He began to rationalize. Drunk drivers killed people all the time, but prohibition was a stupid idea. When's the last time somebody using steroids killed somebody? Well, there was that pro wrestler and his wife, but that could've been depression or something else.

Jomo's intestines felt like they were constricting. He

went to the bathroom and sat on the toilet, staring straight ahead.

All right, he could talk to this guy, but he didn't have to buy. There. He would just talk to the guy. But . . . what if he had a gun? What if he kicked his ass for wasting his time? Christ, the redneck accent—what if he was in the Klan? What if this was a setup? Okay, don't go.

He got off the toilet, stomach still churning. It reminded him of when he was a kid and he was waiting for his parents to dole out punishment for an indiscretion—a couple of swats on the butt, toys taken, lecture, or, if he'd been really bad, a full-on, exposed-butt spanking. He'd gotten only a few of those in his lifetime, like the time he was caught playing down the street without permission. He was seven. His friend Moses lived around the corner. Jomo could go by himself, but only if he asked his mother or father first, and then they'd call Moses's parents to say he was on the way over. Jomo had gone off on his own twice before, and been warned by his frantic parents not to do it again. His butt stung for a bit; the disappointment of his parents was even worse. At least there was closure back then. Now his mind raced. What would his parents do if they found out that Jomo was messing around with drugs?

The *Star Trek* theme went off. Jomo grabbed his cell.

"What!"

"Dang, is that any way to answer the phone?"

It was Miranda. He didn't know what to say. The pause lasted a full three count.

"Jomo. Hello. This is earth. Are you receiving us, Jomo?"

"Yeah, what's up?" Jomo fumbled.

"Sunday dinner—we still on at your place?"

"Um, yeah, yeah. We're having roast beef—"

"Ahhh, sweetness? I'm a vegetarian!" she said. "Isn't this a bit like inviting a conscientious objector to a war?" She giggled and clearly expected Jomo to groan. Jomo tried to refocus; something about veterinarians, right?

"I thought that was funny—"

"What was funny?"

"What was funny?" she said, mocking him. "What's with you?"

"I'm sorry," Jomo said as he sat down in front of his computer. "I'm in the middle of something. Can I call you back?"

Miranda sighed. "Yeah, sure, okay. Not tonight. I've decided to wash my hair, rearrange my MP3 collection, and build a machine that opens a portal between earth, heaven, and hell. I figure God's going to be a bit upset, but hey, this is for science, yo. What do you think?"

"Yeah, yep," Jomo said as he typed in the keywords "anabolic" "steroid" and "synthetic" into Google.

"Then I'm going to take off my clothes, put on some Usher, and do myself while I whisper your name until I pass out. How's that working for you?"

"Good, good," Jomo said as he started reading an e-mail thread on the best ways to beat a drug test. "Okay, great, I miss you too. Got to go."

Jomo walked into the diner and felt immediately out of place. In fact, once he glanced around at the clientele, he felt a bit like an oversized billboard for clean living—football letterman's jacket, multicolored scarf, blue oxford button-down, khaki pants, loafers with black socks—his school uniform. His backpack was slung over his left shoulder.

The joint wasn't in a bad neighborhood. The city's best music store and tattoo parlor, at least according to alt weekly *Seven Days*, were located on Fairfield Avenue. As Jomo had walked up the street, he'd realized it was one of the areas where gentrification hadn't stuck. Winter-barren trees bordered the avenue, with scrapes of grass on postage-stamp-sized yards. Plastic bottles and crushed beer cans shared the gutter with crumpled cigarette packs, wasted bags of fast food, and sooty patches of compacted snow that had iced over. Fairfield was the classic mix of eclectic and dodgy, trashy and arty.

The Eat-Rite was another story. This wasn't a faux dive. The antismoking laws were clearly being flouted. The food looked, well, sketchy.

As he slowly walked toward the back of the restaurant, the only sound above a whisper was the usual staff-cook communication, which included F-bombs, and the tinty blare of the old-school beat box radio that was set to some blathering-on talk radio about illegal aliens and crime.

Jomo guessed that the bald guy in the back of the room was his contact. He was where he'd said he would be—a booth in the back of the restaurant, near the bathroom, away from the windows and facing the front door. Jomo could easily see why he'd been asked to come here.

He was reading *Newsweek*—that seemed nonthreatening. But as Jomo got closer, he saw that the man wore a grayed, faded wife beater shirt, which exposed the Reich eagle, sans swastika, tattoo on his left biceps; on the right biceps was the word *Pride*, spelled out in a runic lettering. Then there were the faded Waffen-SS tats on both sides of his neck. The man sat alone, a white cup—a used tea bag and a squeezed lemon wedge lining the saucer—in front of him.

Jomo took it all in—the Eat-Rite, the man he was coming to see, the tattoos—and he was scared as hell. He nearly walked out—well, backed out—but at that moment the guy looked up and made eye contact.

"Um—," Jomo said haltingly, and walked the rest of the way over to the booth. He stuck out his hand. "I'm . . . Jomo."

"Ganz. Virgil Ganz." Ganz left Jomo's hand hanging and set his magazine to the side. "Sit," he said, motioning.

Jomo stiffened; he wasn't a dog. But he slid into the booth because he didn't know what else to do. Ganz pointed at the waitress, a young woman with an old way about her. She schlepped over.

"You want something? It's on me," Ganz said.

"Uh . . . Coke," Jomo told the waitress, who sighed and slipped away. Ganz sipped on his tea.

"Caffeine'll kill you," Ganz said. "I don't touch the stuff. Green tea. Cleanses the system. Cigs on the other hand—hey, the Indians did just fine with the stuff. Moderation is the key. Moderation in terms of vices."

Ganz pulled away from the table, sat back, and stared at Jomo. Jomo focused on Ganz's biceps. The guy was buff but not a monster.

"You don't sound black on the phone," Ganz said.

"Hunh?"

"You sound, you know, kind of white on the phone?" Ganz said.

"Is that going to be a problem?" Jomo asked tersely before remembering where he was. No Jayson, no backup.

Ganz shrugged and sipped a little more tea.

"I see you eyeing up my tattoos," Ganz said. "Okay, I'll be direct. Yes, the tats are your basic skinhead look."

Jomo's eyes widened: His face went flush. Ganz drained his teacup, lit a cigarette, took a drag, flicked an ash into the empty teacup, and then leaned against the booth back.

"That was then, this is now," Ganz said. "I've seen the light and kneel at the altar of capitalism. I drink of the fruit that is supply and demand. If you've got money, I'm your brother. If you don't, get the fuck away from me."

Ganz paused when the waitress came back with Jomo's soda. She held Jomo's glass just below the lip. Jomo fought the urge to wipe the glass before taking a sip.

Ganz blew a few well-shaped smoke rings that slowly wafted just to the left of Jomo's head. Then his face went deadly serious.

"I was a chemistry major in college," he continued, jabbing the air with his cigarette as he talked. "I got a master's degree in pharmacology, but where the hell was I going to work? Do I look like a fuckin' lab-coat wearin', suburban NASCAR dad to you?"

Jomo wasn't sure if he should smile or not. He knew that he couldn't add anything to the conversation. Unsure what to do, he quickly drank more soda.

Ganz grinned crazily at him.

"And then it hit me—the lucrative but admittedly perilous illegal recreational pharmaceutical industry! I cooked up meth, acid, Ecstasy, whatever. Meth was great, because the fuckin' hillbillies were just crazy for it. But they talked a lot—couldn't be trusted. I had these tweaked-out wrecks showing up at my door at all times of night. I shot at one poor bastard when he wouldn't take no for an answer."

Ganz swept a hand across his scalp and took a breath.

"My God, people would offer sex, sex with their kids, pets, all sorts of crazy shit when they couldn't pay," he continued. "And when the cops busted 'em, they'd sell out anybody and everybody. Some rat did me in, but the cops only got me for a minor distributing rap. I was a small-time dickhead, so instead of jail, I spent some quality time under house arrest. The judge thought that a college-educated kid like myself could be rehabilitated. I told him, 'Yes, sir, with God's help.'" Ganz laughed and fished out a chunk of ice from his water glass, popping it into his mouth.

"It was then that I realized, while processing and unpacking the enormous amount of shit that comes out of the television, that I was in the wrong fuckin' business." He pointed at his head with a lit cigarette. "What business should I have been in?"

Jomo shrugged his shoulders. His stomach was going queasy and he tried not to fart. The more he held it in, the more uncomfortable he felt, and the more he strained to look calm.

"The image business!" Ganz said, his voice growing louder. "Two things. First, everybody wants to look good. We're constantly being told that feeling good begins with looking good. Fat, flabby, out-of-shape people are the real pariahs. They spawn fat kids, and all these fat shits are a drain on the health-care system. I read somewhere that well-educated fat asses are more likely to get screwed out of jobs and promotions. My friend, we're obsessed with beauty and fitness, and we'll go to any length to ensure we look good. If this isn't so, if this isn't the truth, then why are rich bitches willing to squirt botulism into their foreheads? Goddamn, third-world ankle biters die from the same shit American women blast into their bodies to tighten up wrinkles. Fuckin' brilliant."

This guy was too weird for words. Jomo knew he was a nut job, but he was frozen in the chair. Why hadn't he just run out of the place? And was there really such a thing as an ex-skinhead? He wondered if Ganz was not only crazy but possibly murderously nuts. The kind of person whose rage would blow up to a point where he'd pull a gun out of his pants and start shooting up the place—Jomo first. Now he knew what seemingly normal people in bad situations meant when they told police and the media, "I don't know what I was thinking."

Ganz crushed out his cigarette. He chomped more ice.

"Second thing—and this pertains to boys like you—you guys want to be buff, you want to get big, you want muscle mass." He made a point of flexing his own large biceps.

"It's not just athletes, though," he added. "Take a look at rappers. Can you name a fat rapper you take seriously? So why not get into the steroid business? Not just to distribute; I'm talking about designing a quality product."

Was it his turn to talk? Jomo wondered. Swagger, baby. Don't let Ganz think he's jelly.

"All right," Jomo said meekly.

Damn.

"Mmm, how, how . . ." He groped for composure. "Uh, how do I know your stuff is, umm, safe?"

He had to ask. He *had* to. And now he wondered if the question was going to send the crazy man into a tailspin. To his surprise, Ganz grinned.

"Good question," Ganz said, as if he were a car salesman. "No, that's a great question. Here it is."

Ganz raised his shirt and showed off magazine-worthy six-pack abs. "This is my testament. I am not only the president, I'm a client," he said, punching himself in the abdomen. "I am the Sistine-freakin' Chapel."

"Whoa," Jomo said, not unimpressed.

"I take nandrolone; you might know it as Deca," Ganz continued. "A nice anabolic steroid that I've worked on and repackaged. I'm calling it Active X."

"Worked on?" Jomo said, incredulous.

"Yes, no side effects," Ganz retorted. "My cock is still huge—you ain't going to see it neither, freak. Look at my face. No zits. My back, no zits."

"What about, you know, 'roid rage?" Jomo asked, suddenly remembering one of the articles he'd found online the other night.

"I've been pissed off since birth, so I couldn't tell if I do or don't have it," Ganz laughed. "But come on, that's a freakin' myth anyway."

Jomo sat thinking. Ganz was crazy, but he was built like he could go a couple of rounds in a boxing ring. It's how Jomo wanted to remodel himself. He wanted the kind of body that could help dish out pain. He couldn't help his height, but the right body made up for a lot. The combo of brains and body would catch the attention of scouts. No more "cute" Jomo. No more baby-fat Jomo.

"You want some more pop?" the waitress asked as she ambled over. Jomo was glad for the interruption.

"Yes, ma'am. Thank you."

"'Yes, ma'am,'" Ganz said. "'Yes, ma'am!' She's probably thinking, 'Why's that nigger sitting back there with that asshole?' But you hit her with some mock respect." He looked at his watch. "I got 'bidness' to tend—where's my money?"

"You want it right here?" Jomo asked, straining to keep himself from looking suspicious. Was Ganz out of his mind?

"Yeah, nobody gives a shit here."

Jomo pulled a white envelope out of his coat pocket and slid it over to him.

"Nice," Ganz said as he counted the tens and twenties. "An envelope. Very classy. Freakin' rednecktards used to bring in wads of cash. Lint and crap all over it."

Ganz laid a five-dollar bill on the table and motioned for Jomo to follow him out of the restaurant. The two crossed the parking lot and stopped at a pimped-out Chevy pickup. It was a well put together beast of black and chrome, with tinted windows. Ganz opened the door, reached into a gym bag, and pulled out a lunch-size brown paper sack. *That's it?* Jomo thought. *A sack?*

"Here's a twenty-one-day supply," Ganz said, as if he'd read Jomo's mind.

Jomo opened the bag. Inside were several vials of a clear liquid, something that looked like a really thick pen, and a box of needles.

"I—I thought—," Jomo said before looking up from the bag. "I thought there would be syringes and needles."

"Stop watching TV," Ganz said. "It's so simple, even a high school fuck like you should be able to use it without killing yourself."

Ganz reached into the bag and pulled out one of the vials. When he clicked it into the pen like an ink cartridge, a knob popped out of the back of the pen. He opened the box of needles and screwed one into the top of the pen. He pulled off the vial's safety cap.

"Okay, simple," Ganz instructed. "You dial the dose knob until the little number in the window says ten—one zero—no more, no less. This ain't your momma's cookie recipe. I've got this calibrated right."

Then, to Jomo's absolute shock, Ganz lifted up his T-shirt, jammed the needle into his abdomen, and depressed the knob, which steadily moved back into the pen. He put the safety cap back on, unscrewed the vial from the pen, and then dropped the pen back into the bag. Well, at least it looks easy enough, Jomo thought, still hardly believing Ganz stuck himself in public.

"And it's painless," Ganz said, seeming to read Jomo's mind. "You stick it in your abdomen, your upper arm, or your upper thigh. Each cartridge has a seven-day supply. I blew through one day, but, shit, think of it as a worthwhile test. You'll feel the difference sooner than you think. Don't skip a day, and keep a consistent schedule. I'll contact you in two weeks."

"Can I have your number?" Jomo asked. "What if I need—"

"I'll call you!" Ganz said. "I don't need to hear from you. This is easy shit, and you're getting a good price. By the way, you don't say boo to anybody about this or me. You don't tell your friends about this. You don't tell your fuckin' girlfriend, if such a person exists. If I get done, if I feel any heat, no matter how fuckin' mild, you get burned. Understood?"

Jomo nodded. He most certainly understood.

"Well, um, thank you . . . ," Jomo started, sticking out his hand.

Ganz rolled his eyes and walked back to the diner. "Jesus H. Christ, go home," he said over his shoulder. "You'll hear from me."

Jomo jammed the brown paper bag into his backpack and walked away a helluva lot faster than he had arrived.

The next morning, while his father slept on the couch, Jomo emerged from the shower and toweled off, stealing glances at the brown paper sack on the sink. He checked the lock on the door, then brushed his hand over the mirror. He pulled out the pen and popped in a cartridge. He pulled out a needle, screwed it into the pen, and dialed the knob to 10. He pulled off the safety cap.

Jomo looked into the mirror. Once he took the shot, he told himself, there would be no turning back. And he couldn't claim he was naive or peer pressure got to him. That would be a lie. He did this on his own.

It was painless; the shot not matching his anxiety. Jomo put the cap back on, then immediately washed his hands.

"Jomo!" his father bellowed from the bottom of the steps. "Jomo! Do you want tea? I'm also making some scrambled eggs. You want some?"

Shit! Jomo swept everything into the bag and rolled the bag up in his towel.

"Jomo!"

"Yeah, Dad! Tea and eggs. Great! I'll be down in a minute."

He unlocked the door and sprinted to his bedroom, unwrapping the towel and stuffing the bag into a shoe box he'd found in the basement the night before. For a second he thought he heard his father walking up the steps. He panicked, dumping the box behind his headboard, and listened. Nerves, false echoes, ghosts in his head—his father was still downstairs. He dug the shoe box out again and this time placed it in his old gym bag. He carefully stowed that in a small trunk in the back of his closet.

Jomo went commando, throwing on some sweatpants and a Cranmer football T-shirt. Time for his acting job, just in case his dad started asking questions. Don't be a dork, he told himself. Be cool. Be smooth.

"Time to start the day out right, with the breakfast of would-be champions: cholesterol and green tea to balance it out," Jomo chirped. Oh, *that* was smooth, he blasted himself. King Dork.

"What?" Edward said, who was whipping up eggs in a bowl.

"Nothing," Jomo said. "Just talking. You know me."

"I hope you don't mind—we eat late on Sunday during the playoffs," Jomo's father was telling Miranda as they stood by the butcher block in the kitchen. "Those two in there," he said, meaning his brother and Jomo, "well, Gabriel's trumpet could blast a harrowing high C and those two would be too trans-fixed by the game to comment on their impending demise."

"Dad, I'm right here," Jomo said, walking into the room. "The Colts are burying San Diego."

"Ah. So why don't you offer your guest something to drink?"

"That would be nice, Mr. Rodgers. Thank you. A 7UP would be great," Miranda said. "And thank you for having me over for dinner."

Jomo handed her a fresh can. He smiled as his fingers brushed against hers.

"I bet my son didn't tell you that I made a special pasta

dish for you," his father said. "Fresh vegetables and a crème sauce."

"You didn't have to go to the trouble," Miranda protested.

"No trouble at all," Jomo said, turning from the game.

"'No trouble' says the brother who isn't cooking." His father laughed while topping off his wine glass.

"But—" Jomo began.

"Yes, Jomo *did* drag me to Whole Foods, and he insisted on selecting the choicest vegetables for your dish," his father said.

"Jeez, Dad, you gonna tell her how I diced the vegetables next?" Jomo groaned.

"Oh, no, he threw an interception!" his uncle Will yelped from the other room. "The game's getting close."

Jomo looked at Miranda, then at the game. "Ah, I'll be in there." He pointed toward the living room.

"Okay," his father and Miranda said simultaneously. Miranda followed up with "I'll be in in a minute."

Jomo backed up slowly out of the room.

"I'll see you in a minute," he said.

His father took a sip of wine. "So what are your intentions toward my son?" he said in a stern voice.

"Uh, okay, I—"

"Dad!" Jomo protested, but only half-heartedly. If his dad liked someone, he liked to needle and poke. And that meant he liked Miranda, so it was all good.

"I'm kidding, I'm kidding." His father laughed again, opening the oven to look at the pasta primavera. "Would you believe Jomo's mother's father asked me that in all seriousness when I started dating his daughter? I've always wanted to do that. Now my work is done."

"Hey, Miranda, why don't you come in and join the fun part of the family?" Uncle Will shouted from the living room.

Jomo's father shooed her away.

"Mr. Rodgers," Miranda said as she cut a slice of sweet potato pie, "where'd you learn how to cook like this?"

"My mother and my grandmother, my dad's mom," he said, fixing himself a Bombay and tonic.

"Yeah, sure did," Uncle Will cut in. "We both did. Mom and Bessye taught us how to cook, wash our clothes, and iron. They said women in our generation weren't going to put up with lazy-ass—excuse my language—men doing nothing."

Jomo's father nodded, while Uncle Will shoveled a large forkful of pie into his mouth. "And they got that right."

"Here's the thing," Will said, wiping his mouth. "Here's the thing that I've been trying to tell Jomo."

Jomo looked up to the heavens and then glanced at Miranda.

"I've been trying to tell the boy that football will get you a little play," Will said, motioning to his brother for the last of the wine. "But if you want to impress a woman, learn how to cook a good meal and learn how to iron pleats. His father was a good ball player, and so was I, but I swear, we got more action—"

Jomo stared bug-eyed at his uncle, and thankfully, his uncle stopped before he could do any more damage. His father chuckled, and Jomo wondered how he could get through this night without losing his mind and his girlfriend.

"Ah, water. Yes, I need some water," Will said, rising up from the table.

"You used to play football, Mr. Rodgers?" Miranda said, giving Jomo a wink.

"I played a little bit," Jomo's father said, squeezing a wedge of lime into his drink. "But that was way back when I was a young man and had nothing serious to do."

Classic Dad, Jomo thought—took every chance he could to down the game.

"Yep, he was good, too, until he got his butt kicked off the team," Uncle Will added, sitting back down.

"I threw myself off that damn team," Jomo's father retorted.

"Oh, God, do we have to go through this again?" Jomo groaned.

"Hold on," Miranda said. "You got kicked off the football team. Seriously?"

Jomo's father pushed back from the table and hooked his fingers together behind his head.

"I was a junior at Harrison and William here was but a

freshman," he said in a booming voice as if he were narrating a tale. "However, he was already this freaky good player who everybody loved, including Coach John J. Gallas, the dean of the Great Lakes 8 Conference football coaches. I was the brains of the family—"

"You were the geek," Jomo's uncle broke in. "A big brainy geek. Secretly watching *Dr. Who* on Sunday nights—come on now."

"Now who's telling this story?" his dad asked. "I'm telling what's being put down, so you'd better pick up on it."

"Well, I'm just adding the needed context," Will said, nodding righteously.

"Anyway, I was on the team—special teams and a cornerback on nickel packages—"

"That's when there's five defensive backs on the field," Jomo whispered to Miranda.

"Yes, I know. I've actually seen some football games—even on TV," she said. "With sound and everything."

"I see why you like her, son. Shy and retiring—not at all like you. Okay, where was I? Yes, I was on the football team, but I was no longer the rah-rah type."

"He got politicized," Will yelled.

"Yes, I did," Jomo's father shot back. "Particularly around the antiapartheid movement. They were doing something bigger than boozing and bitching about classes. I started going to meetings, then I started speaking, and by the time I was a junior, I was leading demonstrations urging the school to divest its money from companies that did business with the South African government. Well, this didn't make Gallas happy, because the trustees were giving him hell. So he leaned on me and I pushed back, and my already limited playing time was reduced further. It all blew up one day when I came in late for practice—by that time I really didn't care—and I was given an ultimatum: Give up the politics or don't come back. So, I said, 'Forget you, old man,' and left."

"'Forget' wasn't the word you used," Will said, pointing at his brother.

"Whatever word I used, it started with an F, and I was off the team. My dad wasn't too happy. As I remember it, little brother, you weren't too happy either."

"I thought you let the team down," Uncle Will said. Jomo tensed up. This was usually where, in the retelling of stories, his father and uncle got a little hotter under the collar than necessary. "Teams work when all the parts are there." Will sighed.

Jomo's father waved his brother off.

"I need some water," Jomo's uncle said, getting up again. "Can I get anybody anything?"

"No, thank you," Jomo said. He got up and walked over to Miranda, bending over her left shoulder. "Let's go to the living room," he whispered, grabbing her hand. "Thank you for dinner, Dad."

"Yes, it was great," Miranda added.

His father traced a finger around the rim of his tumbler. "Yeah, yeah, my pleasure." He downed what was left in the glass.

"Join us?" Jomo asked, hoping his father would say no—he really wanted a little time to hang out with Miranda.

"I'll be in . . . in a minute," his father said before making himself another drink. "Kind of wish your mom was . . ." He trailed off and wandered into the kitchen.

If this had been just a family get-together, with cousins and great-aunts and uncles sitting around egging his father and uncle on, Jomo would've tuned the discussion out. Tonight, though, it was pissing him off.

Jomo and Miranda settled down on the couch. The sound on the TV was down—a *Simpsons* repeat.

"When it's the Ed and Will show, it gets kind of intense," Jomo explained apologetically, wrapping his arm around Miranda. She laid her head on his shoulder. "I hope they didn't drive you nuts."

"Nah," she said. "You should hear my mom and her sisters. Your uncle kills me. And your dad has been really nice. Dinner was great. But he seems so sad."

Before they could get comfortable, his uncle walked in and over to the bookcase. He opened a large album.

"I didn't want you to think that this was a sad ending," he said, flipping to a photo of Jomo's father as a young man—his brown skin was unlined, the photo picking up the dark freckles on his cheeks. Edward sported a red, green, and black skullcap, an army field jacket, and a red T-shirt adorned with a likeness of Nelson Mandela.

Miranda leaned forward to look; so did Jomo. He barely remembered the picture; he hadn't seen it since he was a kid. He was struck by how young and in love his dad looked. He remembered his mom telling him that his dad would call out other black men for smiling when "other brothers and sister were dying." Militant Ed—that's what they called him. But in this picture he was in love, and it showed on his face. And who wouldn't have been happy to be sitting next to the beautiful young woman beside him. Her skin was darker than his, and she had haunting brown eyes. She wore a simple white sundress with a blue jean jacket. Her feet were bare. Her hair was in ringlets but pushed up high with hairpins.

"My brother's hotheaded, woolly-brained ideas of saving the world apparently captured the heart of a lovely young art student," Jomo's uncle said, crouching in front of Jomo and Miranda to show them.

"She was beautiful," Miranda said, leaning to look. "I mean, she still is."

Jomo's dad shuffled into the room and looked over their shoulders.

"Ancient history," he murmured before sliding down into his recliner. Jomo sized up his father's reaction to the photograph. He never knew when something like a photo or even a scent would trigger a blowup.

"Dad was pretty radical back then," Jomo told Miranda,

hoping to steer the conversation away from his mother.

"Your mom was too," his father said, before twirling his glass and taking a gulp from his Bombay and tonic.

"You were always talking about revolution and solidarity. Changing minds and clearing heads—that's what you used to say, Dad, right?"

His father popped the footrest, but before he could answer, Uncle Will said, "Yeah, yeah, Jomo's parents would protest any injustice, anytime, anywhere. They'd drive up to Chicago or Detroit or down to Indy. Drove our parents silly wondering when he'd get his fool ass killed messing around in other folks' business. How you ever graduated magna cum laude is beyond me."

Miranda scanned the photo again and looked toward Edward.

"So you were a hellraiser *and* kind of hot, Mr. Rodgers," she said.

Jomo's father grunted.

"Do you wish you had stayed on the football team?" she asked.

"No!" screamed Jomo and Will.

"That's not true, that's not true," Edward said, now with a noticeable slur. "It just wasn't fun anymore, like it was when I was kid, you know."

"What do you mean?" Miranda asked, leaning toward him.

"The pros, fine, it's a job and they know the risks and I

respect that, although I'm tired of all the endless hype." He kicked off his shoes. "It's college football. It still leaves a bad taste in my mouth when I see low graduation rates or I see young men who are clearly unprepared for the rigors of college paraded around like gladiators and tossed aside when they screw up."

Will got up from his crouch and laid the album on the coffee table. "I knew what I was getting into when I played, Ed," he said, avoiding eye contact.

"Did you? Did you really?" Jomo's father said, his voice hitting a higher pitch. *Here it comes*, Jomo thought. The tirade continued.

"That bastard Gallas filled your head up with some bull about turning pro." Jomo's father's glass slipped from his fingers and onto the floor. He didn't seem to notice. Jomo glanced at Miranda, who looked as though she were listening intently, but he could only imagine what must be going through her mind.

"Hey, Dad, Miranda's got to—" But his father ranted on.

"Where'd that get you when you were screaming on the ground when your kneecap popped?"

"Dad!" Jomo warned.

"What'd they do for you, little brother?" Edward yelled as his brother's jaw tightened. "Not a damn thing!"

"Dad, come on, like you said, ancient history," Jomo said, getting up.

His father turned to Miranda, who had moved in tight to

Jomo. "They dumped him," he told her. "They snatched up his scholarship when they couldn't use him anymore."

And now he turned back to Will. "And who picked up the pieces? Tell me. And who got you off those damn painkillers? And who put you through the rest of college?"

Will's back stiffened, his lips pursed. He cupped a hand as if he were holding a glass of wine. "Here's to the great Dr. Edward Absolom Rodgers," he said in a mock toast. "The master of everybody's life but his own."

"Well, it's not going to go down like that for Jomo. He's not going to go down like you!"

"Enough!" Jomo shouted, jumping up. "I've heard this all my life. Can't you two go one night without getting in each other's faces?"

"Well, technically, we're at opposite sides of the room," Edward said.

Jomo turned and stared down his father. "Clever, Dad. That didn't work for Mom—"

And as soon as he said it, he wanted to suck the words right back in. No, he wanted to fall through the floor. It was a low blow. His uncle was gaping at him. And now Miranda had seen Circus Rodgers, and Jomo was sure she wasn't coming back.

"Well, on that cheerful note, I'm going to bid you all adieu," Edward said. "Miranda, thank you for coming to our humble home." He pulled himself out of the recliner, then fell butt first to the floor. "Damn," he muttered, as surprised as the rest of them. "I think my legs preceded the rest of my body to sleep." Will rushed over to help, but his brother slapped his hands away. Will bent over anyway, pulling his brother up by his armpits.

"Thank you." Jomo's dad mimed straightening his tie, except he wasn't wearing one. Jomo looked away. Away from his father, away from Miranda, away from Will, away from the scene he couldn't escape. The only one who'd been able to was his mother . . . and now things were even worse.

Jomo nodded to Miranda to follow him into the kitchen, wracking his brains for a way to explain his family's behavior and hoping she wasn't about to run away in horror. Miranda, though, broke the ice.

"Intense," she said, rubbing Jomo's arm.

"Yeah," Jomo said, daring to look at her. "I blame the Scotch-Irish influence in our gene pool."

She tilted her head. The dumbstruck look on her face confirmed that this wasn't the time for his brand of humor, or any humor at all.

"A little massa-was-in-the-quarters joke," he said.

"Ah, yeah, a very little joke," she replied.

"Sorry."

They quietly pulled bowls, plates, glasses, and silverware from the table. While Jomo rinsed and placed items in the dishwasher, Miranda found plastic containers and packed away food in the refrigerator and freezer. The silence between them couldn't be any louder, Jomo thought as he turned on the dishwasher. *Say something, idiot!* But once again, Miranda broke the ice.

"Given what I just saw—and not that the answer means much to me or whatever we have going on, I guess—but why do *you* play football?"

Jomo straightened up and looked her deep in the eyes, and before he even thought about it, he pulled her to him and kissed her. It was a long, wet, slow, passionate kiss. They'd kissed before. One time he'd got under her blouse in the closet at a party. But this felt different. This kiss was some sort of a seal. He thought about it as she wrapped one arm around his head, the other across his back. He didn't even care if his uncle found them, because now he knew: She wasn't going to bail, even after having seen his family's weirdness.

The kiss ended in the way good kisses end: the soft crash of knowing that even the most in-love people can't stay lip locked forever.

"I don't know why," Jomo said, still holding Miranda.

"What? Why what?"

"I don't know why I play now, other than I want to and like to and I think I can play in college if I work hard."

"What's with you and non sequiturs?" she asked, teasingly.

"Hunh?" Jomo said. "Oh, yeah. Funny. Whatever. You asked me about football."

"So you want to be a big man on campus," she said. "Is

that what you want? Be on TV, highlight on ESPN, seventy thousand folks cheering you on, all that."

"Come on, now. You know that's not me," he said, drawing away a little bit. "But if I can get a full ride to a good school, I'd be an idiot not to go that way."

"Oooh, Jomo." She laughed. "I believe you believe that. But let's be serious—you love the attention, too. Hey, I would."

"Okay, yeah, I like the attention," he said, then drew her back to him. "It's not a bad thing. Right now, I really like the attention I'm getting from you."

Virgil Ganz was right. Within a few days, Jomo could feel a change in his body. A few weeks later he felt like a different person. Stronger, much stronger. He crushed through three sets of twelve reps on the leg press as if he were crunching aluminum cans. Psyched, he added more weight and ripped through another twelve reps. Jomo was astounded. But what he really loved was that people were taking notice when he worked out—even the linemen.

Today he sped through his normal leg exercises, doing four sets per machine, adding weight after each rep. When he got to the calf raises, a few teammates crowded around. By the time he finished his fourth set, with a weight twenty pounds more than his previous best, they cheered him.

Jomo fed off the energy.

"You," Jeri said, a mock Austrian accent, pointing at

Jomo. "Ahnold, you're pumped up, but you need to slow down."

"Come on, Jeri, let me do this last rep," he said.

"Fine," she said, picking up his clipboard.

"Just one more . . . And ten!"

"All right," Jeri said, but Jomo ignored her.

"Eleven!" he huffed, jerking back the handle.

As Jomo continued to charge through the reps, Jeri said, "Whoa, whoa, slow down."

"Twelve," he yelled, pulling back the handle one last time, then letting the weights hit the stack loud enough to announce that he was done.

"Whew! Yeah. Can I do another set?" he crowed as he got up from the seat and wiped it down. "Hell yeah, I can do another set," he growled, slamming the towel to the floor, throwing high fives with the guys who were around the machine.

"Jomo, come over to my desk, please," Jeri said angrily.

Jomo followed behind her. What was she getting pissy about? He's working and she wants to talk? About what? But as Jeri stared at Jomo's weight chart, his thoughts took a horrifying 180-degree turn. Was she onto him?

"You've made significant progress," she said, continuing to scan his chart. She set it down and looked directly into Jomo's eyes. She looked more worried than mad.

"You're working hard. But I'm concerned that you're going to burn yourself—"

"That's just it—I'm finally making progress, just like you

said," Jomo explained, feeling exactly like a child covering up to a clueless parent. "And so the harder I go at it, the more progress I'll make. I just want to be the best I can be. I'm committed now."

"And I want to help build you into a solid player, really," she agreed. "But Jomo, if you keep up like this, you're going to get hurt."

"But I feel great," he protested. "You were so right about this. I got two introductory letters from schools, saying that they can't wait to see me play in the fall."

Jeri nodded. "This is good stuff. But Jomo, you don't do legs and arms five days in a row, and you certainly don't do four sets of twelve. That's way too much—"

"But I'm finally getting bigger," he broke in.

"True enough," she agreed. "You're losing that baby fat you carried when you first got here."

"Yeah, I thought I saw an actual ab yesterday," he said.

Jeri laughed. "You know, that's the first joke you've cracked all day," she said. "Even when you got here this morning, you breezed in, didn't rant about the weather or the hour, just got straight to work."

"Like I said, I'm more committed."

"And that's great," she said. "But don't get burned out. That's all I'm saying. You're a funny kid. You're a smart kid, and that's what I like about you. Your lack of complete jock-ishness—"

"Jockishness?" Jomo laughed. "You went to college, right?"

"You know what I mean," she said, smiling. "Just stick to the plan. And by next fall you'll be in the best shape of your life."

Jomo looked at the clock and realized he had the perfect excuse. "I have to study for an English quiz." He stood up. "I'll tone it down. I swear." He held his right hand in the air.

"Cool," she said. "Let's take a look at your plan next month. I'll even pull out the calipers and we can see how well you're doing."

Jomo flashed a thumbs-up and walked away. As he headed for the locker room, he grinned. He smiled in the shower. He smiled as he walked past the coach's office. He smiled all the way to the library. He smiled while he read. He smiled all morning as he felt his head swell with the belief that he would never be caught.

"Craptacular," Jomo announced to the lunch table as he stared at a forkful of brownish lumpiness. "Meat loaf, my ass."

"Yeah, well, don't eat it," Jayson replied, shoveling a massive fork load of meat loaf and mashed potatoes into his mouth. "It ain't that bad, but you always seem to expect lunch to be some four-course dining experience. By the way, how was lifting this morning?"

"How was lifting? You may not have noticed, my good friend, but I've grown," Jomo said. "I've gone and blown up big time. See, I've developed from a hapless young man with small muscles and a contempt for the corruption of amateurism in the now logocentric world of high school athletics to a young man with slightly bigger muscles who wishes to embody the ideal of the twenty-first-century high school athlete. A big man on campus, if you will."

Jomo stood up. Everyone at the table stopped eating and looked at him.

"A shoe contract," Jomo said. "My life, my soul, my heart for a shoe contract."

Jomo noticed that it wasn't only his tablemates looking at him but half the lunchroom, including the faculty table.

"Thank you," Jomo said. "Tomorrow—me, guitar, Zeppelin covers."

"'Stairway'! Woo-hoo," somebody shouted, and the tension broke with sporadic laughter.

"Rodgers, are you high?" someone else shouted.

Jomo bowed, then sat down.

"Did you just make that shit up on the spot?" Burrell asked. "I mean, damn."

"I—" Jomo said before being cut off.

"Had to be scripted," Jayson said. "Why are you so silly? Seriously? All I asked was how lifting went."

"Didn't you hear, dude?" Jomo said. "I was a god. I'm closing in on your personal best on leg press."

"Bullshit," Jayson said.

"No, seriously, I'm within forty pounds—"

"Forty pounds," Jayson said. "Son, you dreamin'."

"You are dreaming," Jomo said. "*You are dreaming*. Don't drop the 'are' and the 'g' of the 'ing' suffix. And no, I'm not dreaming. I'm blowing up. Big! I'm talking 'thug life' buff, yo."

Everyone at the table laughed. Jomo looked toward Harper at the other end.

"I'm blowing up so big that soon I'll surpass Harper as Head Negro in Charge 'round here," he boasted.

Everyone froze.

"Damn, Jomo," Jayson finally said, shaking his head. "Too far, man."

Harper stood up with his tray and walked over to Jomo. He paused and stared him in the eye.

"You think you're so flow, so fly, so fast," Harper said. "But you're not all that funny, my brother. You've got these white folks fooled, but all these crackers just love an Oreo."

Harper turned and stalked off. Within a few minutes the table cleared save for Jomo and Jayson.

"Before you say anything, I'm telling you as your friend— you went too far," Jayson said.

Jomo slammed his hand against the lunch table. "He's been all over my butt since I got here," he said, straining to keep his voice low. "Maybe because I'm light skinned. Maybe because I dated a white girl. I don't know. But fuck him."

"I don't know either," Jayson said, leaning close to Jomo. "Look, man, all I'm saying is that you really need to check yourself on this. You don't like him, which is fine. I'm not all that charmed by him either. But there aren't more than a handful of us here, and we need to stick together."

"Why?" Jomo asked, the volume of his voice dropping to Jayson's level.

"You really have to ask?" Jayson said. "Let's get outa here."

They got up with their trays, emptied them into a bin, and headed outside. It was an unusually warm day for mid-February, so they sat outside on the top grandstand overlooking the football grounds. They still had fifteen minutes before classes resumed—Jomo had a study hall, Jayson had biology.

"So dude, what's up with you, for real? That wasn't too cool what you did with Harper," Jayson said.

Jomo took a big breath, pursed his lips, then blew the air out, hard. He didn't know what had gotten into him. Suddenly he just felt like pissing Harper off, consequences be damned. "Yeah, well, he'll get over it," he finally said.

"It just ain't cool when brothers fight," Jayson pressed. "It doesn't look right."

Jomo was about to tell him to lay the hell off when a voice called out from below them.

"Hey, gents!"

It was Trey. He jumped up and stood on the tier just under theirs.

"Mmm, chocolate pudding," he said, swirling a plastic spoon in a cup. "What are you talking about?"

"Nonayo," Jayson said.

"Nonayo?" Trey asked.

"None of yo' damn business," Jayson said.

Jomo laughed and looked up at the clear sky. It seemed like it had been gray and overcast for weeks.

"Whatever," Trey said. "Hey, did you hear how completely gonzo Jomo was at the early weight-lifting session?"

"What?" Jayson said.

"He was so good that our very beautiful strength coach had to pull him aside," Trey said. "Do you think it's good to have a woman strength trainer? I get way too much wood happening to pay attention."

"Well, well, my boy wasn't just jawing about his abilities after all," Jayson said, nudging Jomo. "Maybe I need to go in the morning and push you a little harder than what those morning scrubs are doing."

Jomo didn't say anything. He kept staring at the sky.

"Oh, yeah, and Coach wants to see you after seventh period," Trey said, pointing at Jomo.

"What for?" Jomo asked, trying to sound casual, but his mind began an instant reel, from *Damn, Jeri figured out the stuff* to *Did someone say something?* to *Do I look paranoid? Dead giveaway*, he told himself. *Act normal. Act normal.*

Trey shrugged.

"What did he look like?" Jomo pressed.

"He looked like McPherson—perpetually pissed," Trey said.

"Oh, damn." Jayson laughed. "That's going to be stuck in my mind for the rest of my life." He looked at his watch. "Time to step to it, son," he said, poking Jomo.

"Don't call me son," Jomo snapped.

"Okay—time to go, bitch." Jayson laughed again. Jomo didn't respond.

"Jesus, Jomo, you look like you're gonna freakin' hurl," Trey said.

"Shut up," Jomo said as he stomped past them.

The nameplate on the large, solid mahogany door read REGINALD I. MCPHERSON; below it were the words ATHLETIC DIRECTOR. However, Jomo knew, as everyone at school did, that his full-time role was football coach.

Jomo hesitated at the door. He rubbed his shirt smooth. He scratched his neck, took a deep breath, and knocked on the door.

"Come," McPherson barked. His shades were drawn; the lamp didn't illuminate much. McPherson sat behind his desk reading papers. Jomo stood at attention. McPherson was an ex-Navy officer and ran the program accordingly.

"How has off-season training been for you, Jomo?" McPherson asked, motioning for him to sit. Jomo instantly felt caught off guard—McPherson usually called his players by their last names. Yet, come to think of it, there were exceptions, like Jayson.

"Good, Coach," Jomo said, making another attempt to

smooth his shirt. He licked his lips. His mouth felt so dry that he could hardly swallow.

The chair was hard and sat just a bit lower than the desk, leaving Jomo looking up. Jomo knew it was an illusion designed to intimidate, and it was effective.

"How do you like the strength training?" McPherson asked, continuing to read. "Jeri putting you boys through your paces?"

"Yes, Coach, she's tough." He wasn't lying. He didn't need to.

McPherson placed the papers back on the desk. He took off his glasses, leaned back in his chair.

"Do you remember the conversation we had about commitment?"

"Yes . . . sir," Jomo said, bracing himself.

"I had three of your teammates come up to me today and say how much you've matured in the weight room," McPherson told him. He gave Jomo an appraising look. "They said you've been getting after it for the last couple of weeks."

"Yes, Coach," Jomo said, all the while wondering who'd been talking and, more important, about *what* exactly.

"I looked at your chart this morning," McPherson said. Jomo's stomach started churning. "You've shown remarkable achievement since starting this plan, particularly in the last couple of weeks. What's up?"

Jomo nodded and smiled weakly. Careful. Careful, he

warned himself. Don't act suspicious. "It's like I told Jeri," he said. "The more I did, the more I could do, and the more I became committed to doing it. Even on mornings when I didn't want to get up, I could feel myself—"

"Pushing yourself harder," McPherson finished for him.

"Yes, Coach," Jomo said. He decided to throw a bone. "I could hear you, uh, telling me that I could be big-time."

McPherson didn't move or change his facial expression, and Jomo feared that he'd gone over the top. But a moment later McPherson leaned forward, folding his hands on his desk and flashing a rare, wry grin.

"This is what I've been trying to get you guys to buy into since day one. Jayson has always understood it, which is why he's going places." McPherson tapped his fingertips to his temples. "But now *you* get it. That's Cranmer football tradition. If you work hard, good things are going to happen. How many times have I told you all that?"

"A lot, Coach," Jomo said. "I guess it's finally sinking in."

"Good man, good man," McPherson said. "There is no reason why you can't be a leader on this team. I can't run plays. And I can't force you all to do anything you don't want to do. But this team needs more leaders. Not just Jayson or Fitzgerald. You can be one of the leaders."

Jomo didn't know what to say except thank you.

The next morning, Jomo took his shower, e-mailed his mother, and wrote a note to Miranda. He pulled out his shoe box, locked the door, and gave himself a shot. He hated Ganz, but he thanked him nonetheless.

"Jomo," his father yelled from down the steps. "Didn't I ask you to clean the microwave?"

Crap, he thought. *If only I had a drug that would make me not give a damn.*

Part III

"...(THE) CHEMICAL PURSUIT OF POWER AND PRESTIGE IS A DANGEROUS GAME."

—From YouthNoise.com,
on the allure of steroids

"Damn," Jomo mumbled as he looked at the phone.
"Come on, come on." He was so fixated on getting a call from
Ganz that he was barely paying attention to his job at the front
desk, where he'd be dispensing balls and games for the next
three hours.

"Yo, yo," a smallish kid was whining.

"What?"

"Yo, man, I wanted Battleship."

"Yeah, and?" Jomo replied.

"Yeah, this is Boggle."

"Boggle is a game, right?"

"Um, yeah, but—"

"Look, I bet you get crap grades and you're a bad speller. . . ."

"You suck," the kid said, shoving the Boggle game back at
Jomo and walking away.

Jomo didn't pay him any mind. Instead he looked at his phone, wishing it would ring. The volunteer from the college seemed amused as she filed papers in a cabinet.

"Hey, can I get a ball?" a girl asked. She pointed at her friend. "We want a basketball."

Jomo picked up the nearest thing to him, which was a volleyball, and set it on the counter.

"A basketball, Jomo!"

"Okay!" Jomo said, tossing a ball on the desk hard enough to bounce off it and onto the floor.

"Ttttth," one of the girls said. "You act like you're on crack."

Before Jomo could respond, his phone rang.

"Yeah," Jomo said into it, not bothering to look at the number.

"Let's talk."

"Hold on," he said, cupping the phone. He glanced toward his uncle's office.

"Uncle Will," he called out. "I need to take this call . . . outside."

The club rules required there be two people at the counter; his uncle would have to take over.

"Who is it?" Will asked.

Jomo gave a quick panicked answer. "Coach."

"Can't you talk to him there at the desk?"

"I can't hear," Jomo pleaded.

"All right, make it quick," Will said, coming out to take Jomo's place.

Jomo jogged outside. It was chilly, but he was wearing a sweatshirt. Kids were running up the ramp to the door. They all waved or said hello as they filed by him, but Jomo turned away toward the wall.

"Yeah," he said, plugging a finger into his open ear.

"You in for another round?"

"Yeah, yeah," Jomo said. "I've got the money—"

"Price went up fifty dollars."

"Wha . . . Why?" Jomo said. Fifty dollars? What's this bullshit, he nearly said out loud.

"Because it's my drug," Ganz shot back.

"I can't afford that," Jomo said, seething.

"Well, that's not my problem, Joe-Moe," Ganz said lightly, accenting the syllables in a southern drawl. The line went dead.

"Oh, shit!" Jomo yelled, pressing to see if the cell had recorded Ganz's number. It hadn't.

"Shit! Shit! Shit!" he said, slamming his hand against the wall. To his amazement, the phone rang.

"Okay, Joe-Moe," Ganz spat, "now we know who's in fucking charge, right?"

Jomo stayed dead silent.

"Say it," Ganz taunted.

Jomo knew exactly what Ganz was doing. He could just see Ganz's smirking face—he had him by the balls. Man, did he want to tell the son of a bitch off. But he forced himself to remember the big picture. He only had to deal with the bastard once every three weeks. He could do that.

"I can't hear you," Ganz taunted.

"You are," Jomo mumbled.

"Say what?

"You are!" *Oh, God, is this what crack addicts go through?* he wondered.

"Fucking-all right!" Ganz yelled. "The price is two hundred bucks for a twenty-one-day supply."

"I've got two hundred dollars," Jomo whispered.

"Jomo! I need you inside." His uncle was tapping him on the shoulder. Jomo fumbled the phone. His heart was racing so hard that he felt it would explode.

"Hold on," Jomo told him.

"Wrap this up—I need you. Now," Will said.

"I'll be in when I get in," Jomo growled.

Will stared at him, as did a couple of kids who were trying to do bike tricks on the ramp.

"Boy," Will said, "you've got ten seconds to get in here, or I'm going to take that as your resignation." He turned his attention to the kids. "I've told you all a million times not to play on here! Get inside or go home!"

Jomo watched his uncle stomp back into the building.

"Um—," Jomo started, the phone back in his ear.

"Meet me at five thirty in the parking lot at Eat-Rite," Ganz said.

The phone went dead.

Jomo ran back inside, but before he could make it behind the desk, his uncle grabbed him by the arm and threw him into his office. He slammed the door and got up in Jomo's face.

"You ain't too old for me to whip your ass." His uncle's voice was dangerously quiet.

"I—," Jomo said.

"I—I . . . nothing. You don't bark at me. I am your uncle and I am your boss. You respect that. You respect *all* of that."

Jomo blinked rapidly.

"I put my butt on the line when I hired you," Will said. "I had to go to the board for this. I told them you wouldn't get special treatment. Until recently your work record has been exemplary. But in the last few weeks you've come in late, you've thrown some attitude to the other staff—"

"I'm sorry—"

"Did I tell you to talk?" Will said. "Don't talk over me."

Jomo looked at the floor. He was screwing up. And for the second time that week he wondered if the shots were messing with his head.

"Jomo," Will said, his voice suddenly calmer. He put his hands on Jomo's shoulders. "You've got to do it better than anybody else, because you're my nephew, my blood. I don't know what's up, but you better get on your J-O-B, today."

Will lifted Jomo's chin, forcing him to make eye contact. "You understand what I'm sayin'?"

Jomo nodded miserably.

"We cool?" his uncle asked, reaching for a knuckle bump.

"Yeah, we're good."

At the end of his shift at five p.m., Jomo said bye to his

uncle, got on his bike, and pedaled to the diner. It was a quick exchange.

As he pedaled home, he concluded that the scene with his uncle was stress. Nothing more. That's why he was buggy. Ganz's stuff was good, even if the inventor was an absolute freak. All he needed to do was relax, keep working, and all would be right. In a few months he would have reached his goal of 180, or at least be really close—solid muscle—and then he would be able to maintain his new form naturally.

"No, really, I'm fine, just a little worried about Dad," Jomo told his mother. He was slowly swiveling in his desk chair, holding his warm cell phone away from his face. They'd talked for twenty minutes, mostly about his father.

"It's more that . . . he's not himself. I've drawn the last three chess games, and we stopped tonight as I was closing in on a win," Jomo told her, trying to give her a sense of what was going on without bringing up the drinking. He wasn't sure why, but he didn't want her to know.

"Have you considered that you're getting better?" his mother asked, sounding amused.

"To be honest, Mom, it wasn't fun. He was yawning so much that he stopped and said he needed to get a nap. I think he's, well, lonely for you." Then he quickly added, "I mean, it's just a guess."

"I know." She sighed. "I try to talk to him, but he doesn't really want to hear it. 'You abandoned the family. . . .'"

"No you didn't!" It drove Jomo nuts when she went there. He didn't think of it as abandonment. It was more like self-preservation.

"And I don't know what to say to him when he says it," she said, her voice sounding defeated. "I keep reminding him that we could've come out here together, but that's not what he wanted . . ."

"Mom—"

". . . and, well, I know it sounds selfish, but dammit, this was my chance to do what I went to school for."

"Mom!" Jomo shouted. He stopped swiveling.

"I was rambling on, right?"

Jomo was quiet. It wasn't so much that she was rambling on but that they had the exact conversation about this every week. Nothing changed except for everyone getting more and more down. But before he could change the subject, his mother did it for him.

"How's this girl you're seeing?"

"It's going all right," he said, unable to keep himself from grinning. "I can't wait for you to meet her over spring break. You're still coming back, right?"

"Yep, got my ticket and everything," she said. "I'll be staying with Onawumi—"

"Onawumi!" She was an old family friend, as near to an elder aunt as he had. "Why can't you stay here?" He could hear himself pouting like a six-year-old; he hoped his mother hadn't.

"Jomo, come on, you're old enough to see that won't work—"

"It would if you two *tried*." Jomo dared to say out loud what he'd been thinking for months. "But that's not what you two want to do—"

"Jomo," his mother said, raising her voice, "I don't like your tone here. This is hard on you, yes, but it's not easy on any of us—"

Jomo's phone beeped.

"Hold on, Mom," he said before clicking over to the other line. "Hello?"

It was Ganz.

"Hold on," Jomo said, clicking over. "Mom, I have to take this."

"Sure—or is this you trying to get off the phone?" she asked.

"No, really, I have to take this. I'll call you as soon as I'm done, okay?"

"Okay, sweetie," she said.

"Love you," he said, clicking over before he could hear her reply.

Jomo braced himself for another bizarro trip through Ganzistan. He felt great, he looked great; and what was best was that no one suspected a thing. It helped that he was no longer worried about his dad finding out. His dad was, every morning, hung over and asleep on the couch. It was getting bad—missed classes, a blown deadline for a book chapter. Jomo thanked God for tenure and his father's reputation, or they might've been out on the street.

"Hello?" He was guarded.

"How're you feeling?" Ganz asked.

"Huh?" Ganz didn't do small talk.

"I take it that you're following my instructions on stacking and what not," Ganz asked. "You feeling good?"

"Yeah, I followed the instructions to the letter, and it's working," Jomo said warily. "Everybody's talking about how intense my workouts are."

"Good, good," Ganz said. "The price for a three-week supply is the same—"

"Cool—"

"Provided that you're interested in taking up an offer."

Jomo caught his breath. Now what?

"I want to know if you're interested in introducing stuff to some of your fellow students—"

"What—," Jomo began to protest.

"Hear me out," Ganz said in a calm voice. "You send me some business, and you save some money."

Buying was one thing, but what Ganz wanted was out of the question. Jomo didn't know what to say.

"No risk, no reward," Ganz remarked. "You've heard of that."

"Yeah," Jomo quickly countered. "And I've also been told not to piss where you work."

"You're already pissing," Ganz said, his voice shifting from friendly to serious. "I'm sure the school would be none too thrilled to know one of their chosen was juicing up."

Jomo resisted the urge to smash his cell phone on his desk. *Chill, Jomo,* he told himself. *This guy's making a threat that he can't afford to keep.*

"I'm just asking, not telling," Ganz said. "I'm not going to fuck your life."

"I'll see you tomorrow," Jomo said, wanting to end the conversation as fast as possible. "Parking lot, five thirty, right?"

"Think about it," Ganz said, and he hung up.

Jomo looked at his computer. The sound was down, so he hadn't heard the incoming IM from Miranda. She was answering a question he'd sent regarding a Friday double date with Jayson and J'Leesa.

"Can't. Family stuff."

Jomo was miffed. There hadn't been family things before.

"Family stuff?"

It took a few seconds to get a reply back.

"Mom, Dad, sisters—family stuff with grandparents."

Before Jomo could reply, Miranda sent across an idea.

"Why don't you come?"

I can't get my schwerve on in front of the family, he thought.

"Puh-lease. Come on, b with me," he begged.

The reply took longer to come back.

"Family. That's the way it's going to be. U got a choice; choose wisely."

Jomo fired back.

"I make time for u. But I can see that's not appreciated."

There was a quick reply.

"What does that mean?"

He pictured the look on her face—a raised eyebrow, pursed lips. Jomo wasn't backing down.

"It means whatever it means," he shot back.

Jomo waited and waited. There was no reply.

"You still there?"

No reply.

"Whatever."

No reply.

Jomo punched the computer keyboard, smashing the center keys to pieces. "Fuck me!" he yelled. "Fuck my whole stupid fucking lousy fucking useless fucking fuck fuck crap fucked life!"

The IM screen flashed. It was Miranda.

"Poor baby, can't live without me, can you? How's Saturday?"

Aside from the creepiness of talking to or meeting with Ganz, Jomo was feeling like things were cool. He and Miranda were solid, even if they weren't going all the way. When they were kissing, he wanted to go farther. Man, she was hot. But he respected her wishes. They shared a friendship, and he knew that was something far more worthwhile than awkwardly bumping naughties.

Sometimes he worried that he'd jumped in too quickly with Ganz . . . sometimes. Maybe he should've sucked down shakes and swallowed pills first. But every guy he knew who took over-the-counter drugs complained that it was bush league—they weren't growing fast enough. And hell, Jomo was pulling in the props even from his coaches.

"Do I detect some swagger?" Jayson had asked him just a few days ago after phys ed class, where Jomo dominated a five-on-five basketball game that included two members of the varsity team, thank you very much.

Yes, Jomo thought, *even he sees it.* Jomo didn't back down. He was physical. And he stopped helping people up off the ground.

And as long as his grades were good, his dad was happy—as happy as his dad ever got lately. His uncle seemed to think that Jomo had finally hit a growth spurt. "Boy, you're blowing up big," he told Jomo. "You and Jayson are going to dominate next year."

Jomo even thought he was getting smarter. He felt it the most in speech class, as demanding a class he had taken this year. And so on the day he was to deliver Gardner's latest assignment, he was psyched.

This wasn't exactly the subject he'd wanted. He'd been assigned torture in the defense of the country. It was a five-minute speech defending the practice; thankfully, his was the last speech of the period. He was doing well in Gardner's class, scoring As on his previous three speeches, each of which increased in length. However, the five-minute speech, with questions, was the big one. Jomo had researched the subject thoroughly. What worried him was: Could he speak convincingly on a subject that he was lukewarm about?

"It would be good for us to remember," Jomo said, leaning toward his audience from the lectern, "that our enemies are bent on destroying us."

He stopped for effect—two beats—then launched into his finale.

"The attacks on September 11, 2001 were carried out by men who did not distinguish Americans as left or right, black or white, compassionate Christians or zealous atheists. No, they killed without remorse; the innocence of the victims did not figure into the equation. It was a sneak attack not meant for gain in a battle for territory or assets, like oil or water. This was a sneak attack in an effort to cause as much damage to Americans as possible. It was sneak attack to destroy the very fabric of who we are and what we represent."

Again, he stopped. He leaned back and surveyed the room. He thought he had them, because all eyes were focused on him. Gardner, who normally scribbled notes from the back of the room, sat with his pen and notebook closed.

"Now, I ask you, is limited use of torture, distasteful though it may be, worth it if the act elicits information for the greater good, in this case—to save lives? Only someone grossly naive to the dangers of the world would say no, thus allowing the death of hundreds or thousands to occur for the defense of the rights of a criminal or criminals. I can't abide by that and neither should you. Thank you."

Gardner never allowed clapping, but from the shaking heads and "all rights" murmured by his classmates, Jomo believed he'd succeeded. He poured himself a glass of water.

"Questions," Gardner asked as he stood up. He looked around. Keefer had one.

"Mr. Keefer," Gardner said. "And please make it a good one."

A few chuckles arose from the room.

"I like the speech," Keefer began, "but you talked about the greater good in your speech. When is the greater good, um, how can I put this. Um, not good—"

Jomo quickly jumped.

"I see what you mean, I think," he said. "I believe actions that protect the nation from harm or, perhaps, destruction are good."

"D'oh!" Gardner blurted out.

Jomo was confused. When Gardner said things like that, it meant that someone had made a mistake.

"Oh, Mr. Rodgers." Gardner sighed. "The internment of American citizens of Japanese descent, no matter how many years ago the family had emigrated to these soils, was done for the greater good." Gardner air quoted "greater good," before folding his arms around his chest. He struck a superior pose.

Jomo looked at the class again. He couldn't discern what his classmates were thinking. He did know that his own sense of victory after his speech was deflating by the second.

"I . . . ," Jomo started, rapidly trying to come up with a response. "I . . . I don't think, um . . ."

A thought struck him.

"I don't know why you're equating internment then to the question of torture today," Jomo said, realizing that he was stalling rather than putting forward a decent defense.

"No, I'm arguing that your use of the greater good in defense of the country can and does lead to some serious problems. It's a philosophical point of view that should be explored. Here's some extra credit for the class, should some of you need the help: Lincoln suspended something called habeas corpus during the Civil War. Tell me why. Two pages by next week."

Jomo continued to look down at his cards, as if he had failed a test. Of course, he knew Gardner did this to everyone. Jomo had hoped he might be the exception.

"Any other questions?" Gardner asked. "Mr. Caldwell."

Jomo looked up.

"Yes. Jomo, do you believe in what you just defended?" Jayson asked.

"Hunh? That's not a question . . ." Jomo looked at Gardner. "Nobody else got this question," Jomo pleaded.

"No one else asked," Gardner quipped.

"Don't get me wrong," Jayson said. "I liked how you delivered the speech, but I want to know if you believe in what you just said."

"I was given an assignment," Jomo said. "I did it. What I believe has nothing to do with anything."

God, that sucked, he thought.

"So, this whole greater good stuff is just stuff?"

"No, I think sometimes"—Jomo was trying to choose his words carefully—"Sometimes, things are done that look bad. . . ."

Jomo stopped. He realized he wasn't looking at anyone. His eyes had been fixed on items that couldn't stare back. He stood up straight, grasped the side of the lectern, and focused his attention back on the room, beginning with making eye contact with Jayson.

"There are times when we as people and we as a country commit ourselves to an action that may seem reckless or, and Mr. Gardner, you'll be pleased that I'm using big words, antithetical to our core beliefs. But sometimes it must be done because the end result will have benefits that make us stronger, and to do nothing would have consequences that aren't acceptable." *Now, take that, Jayson,* he thought.

"Dude, I just wanted to know if you believed this stuff. Because I don't. It might sound naive and childish, but two wrongs don't make a right. You have to live what you profess or your words don't mean a thing. You can't be for human rights one minute, and then torture your enemy the next—"

Before he could go on, the bell rang. Students started gathering books, bags, and coats and shuffling toward the door.

"Good discussion," Gardner boomed. "Nice work on the speech, Mr. Rodgers, particularly since I know your father must've had a fit that you got this assignment. But we've all got to stretch ourselves."

Jomo walked over to Jayson. "Oh, you had to show out," Jomo said with a laugh. "Did I pass your test?"

"You did all right," Jayson said, putting on his letterman

jacket. "I was just trying to push you, dog, like I do on the field."

Yes, but in the classroom, I'm the one with the good grades, Jomo wanted to say, but he didn't.

Jomo rambled across the quad on his way to the bike rack, cramming some CDs he'd bought from a guy in his sixth-period study hall into his already full backpack. He turned the corner and ran directly into Harper, knocking Harper's books out of his hands, scattering papers everywhere. His own bag went flying, a CD case cracking as it hit the walkway. He dropped his bag.

"Idiot!" Harper said. As he squatted to pick up his books, he picked up one of Jomo's CDs, *No Cities Left*, by the Dears.

"Give me that," Jomo said, grabbing at the jewel box.

"The Dears," Harper said. "Sounds just like the kind of gay-ass, white-boy shit you'd listen to."

Jomo snatched the disc out of Harper's hand.

"Gay-ass Oreo shit—" And that was as far as Harper got before Jomo shoved him to the ground. Jomo braced himself for a fight, his legs spread shoulder width, his fists balled up at his sides.

Harper jumped up as fast as he'd fallen.

"You want to the fight, muthafucka?" he yelled. "Let's go, bitch."

Jomo stood still. Harper, who was a hair taller than Jomo and a few pounds heavier, threw the first punch, a right hook. It just missed Jomo's head. Jomo stuffed a body shot to Harper's gut. The sight of Harper staggering back only stoked Jomo's fury. He wanted more. He grabbed Harper's right arm and twisted it behind him.

"Negro, please," Harper blurted out. "Soft ass—"

Jomo didn't hear him, kicking him in the butt. Hard. Harper went flying.

Jomo had never felt such rage, nor such maniacal pleasure. It dawned on him that he'd never actually been in a full-out fight. Sure, he'd been in a few scrapes, mostly in grade school. But now, with the rush of adrenaline coursing through his veins, he felt a sense of rapturous invincibility. He couldn't be stopped.

He lunged toward Harper, but before he got there, he felt two arms bear hug him and lift him away. He broke out of the hold and whipped around to see Jayson.

"What's *wrong* with you?" Jayson cried, grabbing Jomo again to keep him from Harper.

"Get off me, man," Jomo said, trying to thrash his way free. But Jayson held on tighter.

"What's up with you, man?"

"He wanted a fight, so I gave him one, that's what's up." Jomo finally yanked away from Jayson's grip. He swirled around, now ready to take on Jayson. Jayson stared at him as if he had lost his mind.

Jomo blinked, looking back and forth between Harper and his friends.

"I'm not moving until you settle the hell down," Jayson said, ready to block Jomo. And that's when it hit Jomo: He'd completely flipped out. Shit. And as he stood there, chest heaving, he realized he was damn lucky Jayson had come along before he'd done something *really stupid.*

Harper picked up his stuff. He looked at Jomo. For the first time, Jomo saw fear in Harper's eyes. And he had to be honest: It made him feel good. He liked that Harper was scared of him.

When Harper turned the corner, Jomo threw up his arms in triumph à la Rocky.

"Did you see that?" he laughed, bobbing and weaving like a boxer. "Did you see *me?*"

"If I didn't know you, I would've thought you were on crack or you were juicing," Jayson said.

Jomo stopped. He went deadly serious. He felt tight, and another surge went through him. *How dare he question me?* he thought. His face contorted in anger.

"Goddamn, I finally show some initiative in the gym, and here you come accusing me of some bullshit." Jomo turned his back to Jayson, bent over, and yanked up his bag. "Why are you defending him, anyway?" Jomo continued, squatting back down and shoving the CDs into the backpack.

"I'm not," Jayson pleaded. "You're the bigger man. Harper always shoots his mouth off, and you need to be bigger than him. It didn't need to get to this, man."

Jomo furiously jammed the contents of the bag as far down as he could before he zipped it shut. He placed it between his legs, tucked his shirt back into his pants, wiped his face with the sleeve, then flung the backpack up over his right shoulder.

"You could've been kicked off the team if a teacher had come by," Jayson told him.

"Sheeet, Coach says I'm a leader," Jomo said. "He's not going to dump me for some shoving match."

"*Shoving?*" Jayson said, incredulous. "You were trying to kill him."

Jomo started to walk away.

"You're my boy. I'm just trying to look out for you," Jayson called out. Jomo paused.

"I'm a big boy now . . . ," Jomo started, but changed his tone, "No, I'm a fucking man! Harper owes you one." He imagined Jayson with his mouth agape as he watched Jomo stroll away.

Muggy. No, Jomo reconsidered, as he tried to catch his breath. Muggy didn't quite describe it. Muggy sounded almost cute. This was un-freaking-bearable. The moment he walked out of the locker room, he started to sweat. Heat lines shimmered off roads and turf. Even the birds seemed to be flying slower. The only things that thrived in this weather were the mosquitoes. What a way to spend the week of your sixteenth birthday. His driver's test would have to wait. It was hard to concentrate, though the stakes were high.

It was eighty-five degrees, but the humidity and lack of breeze made it feel like it was ninety-five. The heat soaked the shirts of campers, coaches, and scouts alike. Clark State's field was a sea of multicolored shirts, shorts, and football shoes. The one thing the shirts and shorts had in common: the unmistakable overlapping triple-diamond logo of the Mercury shoe company. Every year the company held weeklong regional camps for incoming juniors and seniors, invitation-only affairs during which the best players were taught to throw more accurately, find holes faster, cover receivers tighter, and run more precise routes. Better still, recruiters dropped in to look at athletes in action, getting progress reports on a series of tests like forty times and vertical leaps. The camp counselors were, generally, unaffiliated with schools: current pro-position coaches and ex-players looking for some extra cash and making contacts for future gigs.

"Good run, baby," D'Andre Calhoun yelled to Jayson, who'd just caught the ball in the backfield and dodged and weaved his way to a twenty-yard gain during a seven-on-seven drill. No contact, just two-hand tags.

"Everybody freeze," Calhoun bellowed. "Now look up. It's not that Mr. Caldwell here is fast. We all know that. What made that play is that he anticipates, he reads, he adapts, he overcomes. He turned a little nothing into a big something. That's big-boy football. The rest of y'all look like freshmen."

The players nodded, because Calhoun was something they wanted to be—a college standout and a former pro. Jomo knew he sure did. Calhoun was five foot nine and built like a fireplug; he was an All-Conference safety in college and a two-time All-Pro. Calhoun played seven years in the league, a career that included several knee operations. He was a position coach in the pros before becoming the head coach of the North Texas Rattlers, last year's arena league champs. The players respected him *because* he busted butts, poked chests, and got into people's faces. He made one kid cry for fumbling three successive series of plays. The kid didn't fumble again. Calhoun complimenting anyone was rare. And his magnanimity was rarer.

"Dammit, Helen Keller!" Calhoun ripped into Jomo for bobbling an easy interception on the next play. "No, *she* would've caught the ball," he added.

Jomo looked down and kicked the turf. This pissed his coach off even more.

"Get your hands off your hips!" Calhoun yelled.

Jomo snapped to and got into the huddle. Jayson was off and replaced by Nick Swisher, a senior from Indianapolis.

"Swisher's rolling left—like Jayson did," Jomo said in the huddle.

When the ball was hiked, sure enough, Swisher rolled to the left, and Jomo, who was playing shallow, bolted to him. Swisher caught the ball and dodged one tackler but was leveled by Jomo's forearm to the chest. He wasn't even trying to tag him down. The second Swisher hit the ground, Jomo stood over him and flexed. Swisher tripped Jomo, got up, and spiked the ball near Jomo's head.

"We don't play that in Indy, punk," Swisher yelled, pointing at Jomo.

Jomo popped up and launched himself into Swisher. The two fell to the ground in a kicking, grabbing, grunting mess. Players and coaches jumped in. Jomo felt himself being lifted away.

"Both of you off the field! Now!" Calhoun screamed, grabbing the back of Swisher's shirt. "You two chuckleheads sit out for a while."

"Coach, he's the one who went all ghetto—" Swisher yelled, pointing at Jomo.

"You can't take a hit?" Jomo said, laughing, as he was held back by another coach. "Grow a pair, bitch, and learn to take a hit."

"All right, big man, you're off the field for the rest of the day!" Calhoun yelled, pointing toward the locker room.

Jomo stood, stunned.

"Get off my field!" Calhoun yelled. "And you ain't coming back until I say so."

Jomo wiped the sweat and dirt off his face and meandered over to the sidelines toward Jayson, who was drinking Gatorade.

Jayson started shaking his head, but Jomo brushed past him, stripped off his shirt, and walked toward the locker room.

"Mr. Caldwell in," Calhoun yelled. "Show these boys how it gets done."

Jomo passed the stands where several scouts and recruiters were sitting; even though they weren't supposed to, they cheered and clapped for what turned out to be another spectacular catch and run by Jayson.

"That boy is a bona fide, A-grade football star," Jomo heard one of them say.

"Did you clock his forty time?" another chimed in. "Hell, he'd be one of three fastest players at State right now."

Jomo rolled his eyes. Jayson, Jayson, Jayson, he said to himself as he kept walking. He kicked the locker room door open just to punctuate his frustration.

"Quite a scene out there," a voice said, its southern baritone reverberating off the empty locker room.

Jomo had already showered and dressed in his white Mercury polo shirt and khaki Mercury shorts, and was lacing up his black Mercury shoes, when he looked up and saw a tall, muscular gentleman with a tanned, leathery face. His salt-and-pepper hair was slicked back.

"Yeah, well," Jomo said, and sheepishly shrugged his shoulders.

The man stuck out his hand out for a shake.

"Helluva hit though," he said. "You popped his ass but good."

Jomo shook the man's hand and started packing his work-out clothes in a white laundry bag with the Mercury logo.

"Jomo," the man started. "Can I call you Jomo?"

"That's my name," Jomo said, but he caught himself being cocky. "Yes. Jomo's fine."

"I'm Hank Stallings, associate head coach and defensive backs coach at Mississippi Tech. The Cavaliers. You've probably seen us play, know our coach, our reputation."

Jomo nodded, telling himself not to bring up the intense

southern heat or the fact that some of the school's fans still waved the Confederate flag at games.

"We don't rebuild, son. We reload, and I think you've got the fire it takes to be a Cavalier. By the way, if anyone asks, I'm here taking a piss, right?" he said, winking at Jomo.

Jomo tried to keep a poker face; he was flattered and amused at the thought of his parents' brains exploding at seeing their son suit up for a university where fraternities and sororities threw balls at which they dressed in antebellum costumes.

"Aren't you on probation?"

"Well, um, yes," Stallings said, throwing his foot on the bench Jomo was sitting on. "But it's only a loss of a couple of scholarships for a year, and we're still bowl eligible and TV crazy. We've got at least one Thursday primetime showdown and two Saturday-afternoon games that'll have a big national audience. Our boys get seen, and some of them play on Sundays."

Jomo continued to pack his gear. *Poker face,* he told himself. *Poker face. Wait,* he thought, *I don't even play poker.*

"Let me get to the point, Jomo," he said. "I've looked at the numbers you've posted. Small, but built. They say you put on twenty pounds of muscle since the end of last season."

Jomo nodded.

"Damn, son, you're serious. I'm serious. I want to see you kickin' ass for the Cavs."

"Well, what does the school have?"

"We're remodeling our stadium, for one, going from forty thousand to sixty thousand with glassed luxury boxes. We've already sunk several million into a new sports complex, which includes state-of-the-art everything, from the weight rooms—yes, rooms—to bathrooms. When it comes to football, we can't be beat."

"And what about the school? Classes. Majors."

"We've got tutors—pretty ones, too." Stallings guffawed. "We'll get you through it. You go to a fancy prep school, right? Cram-something."

"Cranmer," Jomo said.

"Yeah, and that teammate of yours, Caldwell, he's something else," Stallings said. "I'd love to get you both down to Biloxi."

"Jayson, yeah, he's been getting calls and letters and stuff from colleges for a while." Jomo laughed. "I try to keep him from going overboard."

"So how'd the two of you get into a fancy prep school like that?" Stallings asked.

Jomo thought it a condescending question, but he determined to be pleasant, even witty.

"Test scores. Wit. Good looks," Jomo quipped. "But I think the blue blazer I wore for my interview put me over the top."

"Uh-huh," Stallings said. "So I bet your mommas work real hard to keep you there."

"What?" Jomo was suddenly on hyperalert.

"I'm sure your momma works awful hard to keep you in that school, right?"

"My mother's in Seattle—and yes, she's working hard to keep me in school."

"So, I guess then you live with your grandmomma or an auntie, right?"

"Huh?"

"I took a class on the sociology of the black family, y'know, as a way to get to know my boys and communicate at their level, so I know how it is with you kids."

Jomo could feel himself going from uncomfortable to apoplexy. Stallings didn't seem to notice.

"A lot of my boys," he continued, "come from the projects, broken homes, and have a hard time in life. I like to think that they look at me like a father—"

"I have a father," Jomo said through clenched teeth.

"Good. Good. It's so important for young black boys, to have a father to teach 'em how to grow up to be men. You're ahead in the game of life. You know, I have no doubt in my mind that I can turn you into a big-time hitter, maybe even somebody who can make it to the pros. You can get that big payday, buy your daddy a house. Would he like that? Would he like a house?"

"He has a house," Jomo said tersely. What a presumptuous asshole. He slung his laundry bag over his shoulder and headed toward the door.

"Good for him," Stallings said. "I'll be in touch. I'd like to see you and that friend of yours playing for Tech."

Yeah, right, Jomo muttered as he stormed out of the room.

• • •

Jomo sucked down the rest of his chocolate shake and let out a belch.

"Damn, dude, why?" Jayson laughed.

Jomo realized that he'd been too loud and drawn the attention of a few diners in the food court of the Vincennes Regional Mall, including two girls at a table near them who giggled. Thursday was the one night the Mercury campers had off. In two days they'd be headed home with carloads of swag and, hopefully, contacts.

"Anyway," Jomo started, "he's going on about how his *boys* see him as a father figure. And how he thinks if I play for him, I can play in the pros and 'buy my daddy a house.'"

"What, you in the pros?" Jayson said. "He must've been out in the sun too long."

"I know, I know, it took everything I had to keep from just laughing out loud," Jomo said. "He even talked about you. A twofer deal."

"Man, I'm not going down south," Jayson howled.

Jomo laughed too. "Come on, if Alabama or Florida or Georgia came calling—"

"I've gotten letters and whatnot," Jayson said. "I'm not going. Mom is always going on about how backward and racist it is."

"Yeah, but I was in Georgia a couple of years ago, and it was actually kind of cool, especially Atlanta." Jomo suddenly leaned in across the table. "Yo, are those girls looking at us?"

Jayson stole a sideways glance.

"Don't give it away," Jomo hissed.

"It's been given away," Jayson said. "Yeah, I think they're interested. I'm not. And you ain't either."

"I know, I know, but stuff like this never happens to me."

Jomo looked directly at the girls. They were cute, one blond, one a redhead. He waved them over. To his surprise, they responded. There was an awkward silence, as Jomo hoped Jayson would do what he did best: say something smooth. He didn't.

"Y'all are with the football camp, right?" the blond girl said.

"Yeah—how could you tell?"

"Well, you're dressed head-to-toe in Mercury stuff," she said. "Plus there aren't a lot of, how do I put this, *boys from the 'hood* around here."

Jayson closed his eyes and laughed. "Huh?" Jomo asked before he caught the meaning. "Yeah, well, we're from the Fort," he added as the girls sat down. Jomo noticed that an older couple who had been talking a few tables away abruptly left. Were they done, or were they upset?

April, the blonde, and Brittney, her "best friend since forever," talked music, school, even a little football. Jayson, who Jomo thought sucked at the whole wingman routine, did his best to chitchat with Brittney. Jomo liked the attention from April, short and slender with a straight blond bob that partially covered her green eyes. She was sweet and cute and would do. He slid his hand into his jeans pocket and turned off his cell phone.

The four talked until a group of players walked by and sat down. Sensing Jayson's lack of interest, Brittney immediately struck up a conversation with one of them and decided to go to the movies with that group.

"I'm going to turn in, dog," Jayson said, watching her go. "You going to hang out?"

Jomo looked at April. She looked at him. He placed his hand on her thigh underneath the table. She didn't flinch.

"Yeah, we're going to hang out."

"April, do you mind if I talk to Jomo for a moment?"

Jayson motioned Jomo away from the table and out of earshot. He folded his arms and gave Jomo a steady gaze.

"Yo, Jomo, I'm not trying to get in your business, but—"

"But—"

"You're not married, but brother, come on, is she worth it?"

"What, because she's white?"

"I don't care if she was Beyoncé, Jomo—this isn't right," Jayson said. "This isn't you."

"I'm not married, and I don't need permission," Jomo snapped. "We're just hanging."

Jayson looked at April, who was on her cell phone.

"Well, hang then," Jayson said.

"Come on, this is harmless," Jomo said. He held out his fist to bump knuckles. Jayson touched back, but lightly.

"Curfew is ten thirty—don't blow this up, Jomo," Jayson whispered before turning back to April.

"It was nice meeting you," he told her. "Try and make sure the boy gets back home in one piece."

Jomo and April toured the mall, sauntering around chatting. He boasted; she flirted. She talked of her tedious life in "the sticks," and Jomo tried to listen. He nodded when he should, said "Uh-hunh" at all the appropriate moments, but all he could think about was getting her alone.

"I hope to get a scholarship to play football," he told her as they picked through the racks at Dillard's. "But if I don't, I've got good grades, and college is a given in my family. What about you?"

She was quiet for a moment.

"Well, I'm thinking . . . I'm not sure, you know?" she said, pulling a pair of jeans off the rack. "I've thought about journalism, maybe. IU has a great program. So does Ball State. That's probably where I'm going to go."

She held the pair of jeans to her body and looked at them in the mirror. It was then that Jomo realized that two sales associates had been shadowing them through the women's department. It pissed him off.

"I'm bored with small-town life." April, oblivious to the scene, rambled on. "It's so boring down here. We scoop the loop—"

"Scoop the loop?"

She waved a hand dismissively. "Kids get in cars and drive the downtown loop," she said. "It's so cheesy. I mean, why don't we all hang out at the malt shop and sing songs from *High School Musical?*"

Jomo laughed. Her sense of humor reminded him of— He tried to shake that thought out of his head.

"Can we go somewhere else?" he asked, staring at one of the clerks, who scurried back behind the counter.

The two worked their way to April's car, a blue Chevy Aveo with a sticker of Calvin, from the cartoon *Calvin and Hobbes*, pissing on the number 24, Jeff Gordon.

"You into racing?" he asked.

"Oh, yeah. Around here it's religion," she said, sliding into the driver's seat.

"Let me guess—you're a big fan of Tony Stewart."

"You know it," she said. "Indiana guy. And he's cute. You know, that gruff, tough sort of sexy."

Jomo shook his head. "What's up with girls and bad boys?"

"Well, you're kind of bad."

Jomo smiled. "Not hardly." He didn't look at her.

"Not a bad boy, but you're into some mischief. I can tell," she said. "I'll give you the tour, which is free, because there ain't a lot to see."

The two rode around town as daylight gave way to dusk, and Jomo got the tour of fast-food chains and theme restaurants, curio shops and boarded-up stores, picket fences and historical markers, the wrong side of the tracks and rusted-out factories. They even scooped the loop, which, at this time of day, was devoid of kids. Just as well, Jomo thought. He wasn't interested in hanging out with too many locals.

"It's pretty standard, you know," she said, pointing to the street she lived on, a row of small, well-maintained ranch houses shaded by a string of tall oaks. Jomo didn't have to ask why they didn't park in front of her house. "My dad works for the county, construction. My mom is your classic homemaker. My brother is your classic dork."

She took off again.

"So what else can one do in Clark Pointe?" Jomo asked.

April paused. "I know," she finally said happily. "I can show you the best view in town."

They arrived at an overlook above the Wabash River. The solitude of the area was broken by hip-hop and country music. Jomo was nervous, and he could tell that she was too, because they were literally running out of reasons to talk.

"Jomo?" she asked, as Jomo prattled on about music.

"Er, yeah." He strained to find the right thing to say. "Yeah."

"Why haven't you tried to kiss me?"

"I was going to get there," he assured her. So he did.

He kissed her. At first light, then deep and full. He kissed her until they decided to explore this fling with a lifted polo shirt, an unbuttoned blouse, an unhooked bra, some slow jams on the radio, and sweat. And in the heat of the moment, Jomo stopped. He pulled back to the passenger window and stared out at nothing. He didn't see Miranda, but he felt her, smelled her, heard her.

"Wha—," April said, pressing her hands against his chest, then against his cheeks. He turned toward her.

"It's just one night," she said. "She doesn't need to know."

"How did you know?"

"The look on your face," she said, more kindly than he knew he deserved. "Kinda like my little brother when he's done something stupid."

Jomo looked at April, then looked back outside.

"I'm sorry," he said. "I—"

"Yeah, I know," she said.

The uncomfortable silence lasted a minute. April buttoned her blouse, and Jomo pulled down his shirt. She pulled her hair back and clipped it with a barrette that was on the dash. Then she turned the ignition and hit the gas.

They drove back the way they'd come, Jomo recalling the sights as if the car were trying to go back in time to erase the scene.

"You know, I've never gone that far—with a black guy," April told him. "I guess that's why I liked you, because you don't act, you know, 'ghetto.'"

"Goddamn, what in the hell is it today with white folks and the word 'ghetto'?" he cried out.

She touched his arm. "I mean, you know, you're not a thug. That's not a bad thing. It's a compliment."

"Ha!"

"What does that mean?"

"It means that we, I—I shouldn't have been screwing around with some white girl," Jomo shot back. "I shouldn't have let Li'l Jomo run the show—"

"I'm not some ho—"

"I didn't call you a ho—"

"But that's what you meant—"

"And what did you mean by me not being *ghetto*?" he yelled. "Is that some damn euphemism for nigger?"

"Screw you!"

"Not tonight, baby." Jomo slammed his fist against the car door.

"Oh, crap!"

"Wha—"

"Shut up—there's a cop behind us!" she said, exasperated. "Crap!" she said again, banging on the steering wheel.

The cruiser's siren wailed and a harsh floodlight lit up the car. April quickly pulled over and turned off the engine.

"Move!" she hissed, reaching past Jomo to open her glove compartment. She pulled out the car's registration, then pawed through her purse until she found her driver's license. "My dad's going to kill me," she said, fumbling the zipper of her pocketbook. "Damn, damn, dammit."

The officer waited for thirty seconds before he walked up to April's side of the car. He flashed his Maglite through the window toward Jomo's side of the car.

"Ma'am, are you all right?" the officer asked. *What kind of question is that?* Jomo wondered.

"I—," she started.

The officer didn't wait to hear her answer. "Young man, put your hands on the dashboard so I can see them." The cop's tone was all business, if not slightly menacing. *What the hell?* Jomo's mind began to scramble and he froze. His experience with the law had been limited to visits by McGruff and touring the police station when he was a Boy Scout.

"Now!" the officer ordered. It snapped Jomo back, and he dutifully placed his hands on the dashboard.

"Did we do something wrong, sir?" April asked, polite as could be.

The officer didn't respond. Jomo closed his eyes. His mind skittered to lectures from his father about ancient Indiana history—lynchings, beatings, disappearances, and the Klan's second rising back in the 1920s. Then it was like a million years ago. It all seemed real now. His legs began to tingle. He thought about his mother. He prayed the Lord was watching over him and thought about how much he missed church. He suddenly had to pee.

The officer turned off his flashlight, but the floodlight from the cruiser was still on.

"You with that Mercury camp up at Clark State?" the officer asked.

"Yes, yes sir," Jomo said meekly. He was scared, but he

was also disgusted by his own fear. *Yes, yes sir.* A real brother wouldn't be so compliant.

"Uh-huh," the officer said. It was about this time that Jomo noticed in the side mirror a second officer standing by the passenger's side rear door. Jomo looked down to the floor.

"Clearly you're not from around here," the first officer said.

"No, I'm from—"

"I don't care where you're from."

The first officer stepped back from the car and started talking into his clip-on radio. The second officer maintained his station.

"I clocked you going five miles per hour over the posted speed limit. I'm giving you a verbal warning," the first officer said to April. He leaned into the car and looked at Jomo. "Best you be gettin' back to where you're supposed to be," he continued. Jomo nodded.

"And young lady, I think you ought to be headin' right on home after you drop him off," the first officer told April. "We'll follow you over to the university."

Jomo watched them get in their cruiser. April sighed, turned on the ignition, and slowly drove away with the officers in tow. The dorms were only a three blocks away, and they said not a word until she stopped.

"Um, I—," Jomo started, licking his lips.

"I think you should just go," she said, not making eye contact.

April did wait to see Jomo into the building. Again, Jomo thought this was a kindness he didn't deserve but was grateful for it, especially when the officers inexplicably turned their cruiser floodlight on him when he reached the dorm door. Jomo pressed the numbers in the keypad and walked dejectedly into the building.

"It's an old story around here," a voice said as Jomo leaned against the closed door and shut his eyes. Startled, he looked around. It was Calhoun. "Black boy, white girl, bunch of bull."

Jomo couldn't come up with a single response. Indeed, all he wanted to do was to rip the door off the hinges and hurl it at the nearest police car.

"Am I in trouble?" Jomo asked.

"You're not the first one this has happened to," Calhoun said. "To be honest, the cops around here don't like anybody from the camp—black or white." He slapped Jomo on the shoulder. "I'll see you in the morning, on the field, and no bullshit, right?"

Jomo nodded and headed toward his room.

"Yo, man, I—," Jayson asked when Jomo walked in.

Jomo sat on his bed. He pulled off his sneakers, then looked over at Jayson.

"What year is it?" he asked, falling back against his pillow.

The next morning Jomo found himself in a zone. He was physical when he needed to be, and he apologized to Swisher.

Even Calhoun was impressed. But then at lunch he got a call from Ganz. It wasn't the right time or place to do business, so he got him to call back when he would be in a place to talk.

"That camp, whatever, that go all right for you?" Ganz asked, his voice fading in and out on Jomo's cell.

"It was good," Jomo said, keeping his voice low despite the fact that he was sitting in the deserted glass press box above the university's football field. "You know, my time in the forty and vertical leaps were great—"

"How'd you keep them from finding out?" Ganz interrupted.

"I keep it in my bag—they never check," he said. "I take the shot when Jayson is out for a morning run. He's like clockwork."

"You ready for some more?"

"I want to talk to you about that," Jomo said. "You said there would be no side effects—"

"Side effects? What side effects?" Ganz said. "If you've got zits, stop eating pizza and shit."

"No, no! Nothing like that," Jomo said. "I mean, I don't feel like me. I'm doing and acting and saying stuff. You know what I mean?"

"Er, no, I don't know. What the hell are you talking about?"

"I nearly cheated on my girlfriend—"

"So—"

"I get into fights, and I say stuff that I wouldn't normally say, even if I was thinking it," Jomo said, his voice, he knew, sounding ever more desperate.

"Look, kid, I'm not your shrink."

"Yeah, but could it be—"

"What it could be is that now that you're a big man, your inner asshole is finally coming forward," Ganz said.

"But even you said you didn't know if this stuff does something to your head—"

"Listen, JOE-MOE, you don't have to buy from me, but when you look at your well-cut ass in a mirror at camp, ask yourself if you'd even be down there at that camp if it hadn't been for me. Fuck no. Matter of fact, I don't need you—"

"All right, I'm sorry," Jomo said. "I'm out of my mind. I'm tired—"

Beep, beep. It was Jomo's call-waiting signal.

"I'm not feeling—"

Beep, beep. Dammit!

"Can I take this?" Jomo asked.

"Make it fast."

He clicked over.

"Hey, babe. Where were you last night?" It was Miranda.

"Oh, hi, yeah, I was out with the guys," Jomo said, forcing enthusiasm into his voice.

"What, so you didn't want them to know you had a girl-friend?" she said in a teasing way. "Were you squeezing up on some low-rent hoochie?"

Jomo froze. This was *not* the conversation he wanted to be having right now.

"Whatever," he said, feeling irritated and guilty. "I'm really, really busy. I'll call you back." He clicked back over to Ganz.

"Um, I'm sorry about that," Jomo told him.

He didn't hear anything.

"Hello?"

"The price is now three hundred," Ganz said.

"What?"

"Three hundred bucks. Supply and demand."

"I can't afford that!" Three hundred dollars? Was Ganz out his mind?

"Well, it's been nice working with you, kid," Ganz said. "There's plenty of shit on the market, and if you're worried about side effects, well, you're really going to be freaking out."

"Can't we work something—"

"No cash, no good stuff. It's just that simple."

"Come on, Ganz," Jomo said.

Ganz waited for a moment. Jomo knew, he just knew, what was coming next. He was being set up. And sure enough, Ganz said, ever so casually, "Okay then, you can work for me. You bring me customers, and I'll supply you—"

"I don't know—"

"That's the deal," Ganz said.

"Selling?"

"No, just introducing, sending folks my way," Ganz said.

"I'll count to three, and you give me the right answer on three or you'll never hear from me again.

"One."

It's one thing to take the stuff. It's another to be a seller.

"Two."

Is this even a felony? People can make up their own minds.

"Thr—"

"Dammit! I'm in," Jomo said. "I'm in." He exhaled. "What do I need to do?"

"Kid, this is the easiest job you'll ever have," Ganz said. "All you need to do is bring customers to me. Give me some phone numbers and I'll handle the rest."

Jomo thought about people who might want to try what Ganz had to offer. Certainly not Jayson. In the first place, he didn't need it. Also, Jomo knew Jayson would be all over him if he even suspected he was using it.

A few days after the Mercury camp, Jomo made a point of working out at the same time as Trey. As they wiped down the free weights they'd been using, Jomo said, "I'm starving. Wanna grab a bagel? Besides, I want to run something by you."

"Cool," Trey said. "Man, you're like killing me through these sets. It's like something got switched on inside you."

Jomo nodded. This might be an easier sale than he thought.

It was midmorning, and the café was nearly empty. They

sat outside and drank sugar-free raspberry Italian sodas. They munched on everything bagels.

"So, what's up?" Trey asked.

Jomo looked around as if he were being followed and bugged by the Drug Enforcement Agency.

"Seriously, dude, you're creeping me out." Trey laughed. "Is Miranda pregnant?"

Jomo couldn't keep from laughing. "No, you idiot." He scanned again, leaned in to Trey, and said, "I going to tell you something, and I don't want it to go farther than this table. And I've got shit on you, including your occasional bouts with the chronic."

Trey was taken aback. "What the fuck are you going on about, Jomo?"

"You asked me how I was getting big fast," he began. "I'll be honest—I've been taking a new kind of anabolic steroid."

There, he dropped it like a bomb. He got the reaction he thought he was going to get.

"Holy shit," Trey said.

"Did you suspect anything?" Jomo asked.

"Hell no! No way. You're shitting me, right?

Jomo took a sip from his can, pulled down his sunglasses, and leaned back in his chair.

"Little Jomo," Trey said. "Little never-do-anything-bad Jomo. How did you—"

"I made contact with this guy through somebody else—"

"Somebody from the team?"

Jomo paused. Now, he'd known Trey since they were in Cranmer's middle school together. They were friends, but he wasn't close to Trey like he was to Jayson. Jomo decided he'd give Trey only the information he needed.

"Does it matter?" he asked defiantly. Trey shrugged, but Jomo knew he was flashing through possible links.

"Anyway, the stuff is safe," Jomo said. "No side effects, and you've seen the results."

"Jomo, I can't believe . . . ," Trey said, before a grin came over his face. "God, you don't smoke pot, you're not a big partier."

"Well." Jomo smiled before taking another sip. "Are you disappointed?"

"No, not really," Trey said. "I mean, other guys have got to be doing it and keeping it a secret. I just never suspected you."

"Other guys?"

"Like Fitzie," Trey said, spreading some peanut butter on his bagel. "I know he was taking speed last year. God, he was awesome, no fear. I thought you knew. You guys are tight, right?"

Trey bit into his bagel as Jomo put down his own in shock. Fitzie? Fitzie speeding? *Figures*, Jomo thought. And yet Fitzie, the walking health store, the kid with the backdoor contacts, was hailed by McPherson and coaches as the model Cranmer man.

"He offered to hook me up, sounded sketchy," Trey said

before wiping peanut butter from his chin. "You know, there was a guy on the golf team in my brother's senior class—I'll save the name to protect the less than innocent. . . . He used this beta blocker called Propo-something or other. Anyway, he gulped that stuff down to steady his hands. He tied for second in State that year; his best finish before was, like, top ten regional. My brother said his dad was giving it to him—and the coach knew."

"What about you?" Jomo probed.

"Me?"

"Yeah, have you ever taken anything—besides creatine?"

"Not really," he said. "It's been okay. Hey, when I was a kid, my dad got me—damn I thought you knew this—my dad got me some growth hormone shots."

"No shit," Jomo said.

"I shit you not." Trey laughed. "I was like really short in fifth grade. I was born with the runt gene. I still had a cannon for an arm. So, for Christmas—I swear to God I'm not making this up—my dad got me on these growth hormones. It was all hush-hush at the doctor's office. But I grew like four inches real quick. Growth spurt and vitamins—that's what we told people."

"Would you be interested in talking to my guy?" Jomo said, beginning his pitch. "I'm only telling you because it's so effective."

It took ten minutes to get Trey. In another week he'd hooked Calvin Reynolds into the loop.

Part IV

"SUCCESS WITHOUT HONOR IS AN UNSEASONED DISH; IT WILL SATISFY YOUR HUNGER BUT IT WON'T TASTE GOOD."

—Joe Paterno,
college football coach

Greg Hyatt

Prep Sports News and Notes Column

Star-Review

Kudos to Cranmer and Reginald McPherson for requiring its student athletes to submit to drug tests before taking the field for the Colonels. The Hoosier Interscholastic Athletics Association should require this for all students. The HIAA has been lulled into the classic civil-libertarian response that doing so would be an invasion of privacy. Yeah, yeah, blah, blah. Do we want scholastic athletics to wind up having the same issues that pro and college sports suffer through? As we've all seen in stories coming out of Texas, California, and Florida, performance-enhancing drugs have worked down to the high school level, leaving a trail of pain and, in a few cases, death for young men and women who thought they were invincible to the side effects. Worse still are coaches who turn a blind eye to the obvious: kids who took the shortcut from bony to behemoth. Unlike many coaches in the state, McPherson isn't hiding his head in the sand. He's taken the opportunity to lead by example, and he hasn't made a big deal about the school's drug testing policy. Well, Coach, kudos to you for trying to keep Indiana high school football free and clear of drugs and juiced-up players.

"It looks mighty hot out there," the voice-over from the TV studio said.

"That's right, Michelle," said the young blond man with the microphone. Standing behind him was the Cranmer Colonels football team. McPherson stood beside him. "But this is the kind of weather you'd expect for the first day of two-a-day football practices in the area, including here at the Cranmer School, where the Colonels enter the season ranked fourth in Indiana's Class 3A, their highest preseason ranking in seven years."

The team roared behind him. The sports reporter smiled and tried to speak over the boys. McPherson remained straight faced.

"I'll talk with Coach Reginald McPherson in sports," the reporter said. "You're watching the Noonday Report on WSUM-TV, channel four."

The field producer held up her right hand and lowered her thumb and fingers until all that was left was her index finger. Then she pointed to the sports reporter, who'd been asked about the weather again.

"Oh, it's a hot one today, Michelle," he said. "But then, if it was cool, two-a-days wouldn't be good preparation for the season, right, Coach?"

McPherson nodded. By this time the team was doing its drills on the practice field. However, Jayson, Jomo, Casey Fitzgerald, and Trey McBride remained standing behind McPherson.

"Excellent," the reporter said. "Coach McPherson, you're starting many juniors this year; they're battle tested. The polls are confident of this team's abilities—are you?"

"It's early and polls are often wrong," McPherson said, his words measured and steady. "We were young last year, and while we're battle tested, the proof is whether or not we've learned anything from that experience."

The reporter pulled the mike off McPherson and stepped over to Jayson.

"One of the team's captains this year is Jayson Caldwell," the reporter said. "It's an honor not often bestowed on a junior at Cranmer, and you're also a preseason favorite for the All-State team."

"Yeah, um, yes," Jayson said in a halting voice. "It is an honor, and I hope to live up to Coach's expectations."

"The other captain is senior linebacker Casey Fitzgerald.

Any thoughts on the new season?" the reporter asked, turning to Fitzie.

"Coach is right when he said that we've got to learn from last year, and I know we will," Fitzie said. "We're hungry, and we're smarter. And with teammates like my man Jayson, and Jomo and Trey here, we're fixing to get Cranmer to State."

Jomo and Trey smiled. McPherson's face was tight.

"That's Jomo Rodgers and Will 'Trey' McBride," the reporter said. "Trey, you've always been a big kid, but Jomo, you look like you've gone hardcore over the summer."

"Yeah, Coach set up an off-season weight-lifting program," he said. "I wasn't a gym guy before, but now the benefits are obvious." He flexed his muscles like Charles Atlas on the beach. Everyone laughed.

The reporter switched back to McPherson.

"Coach, you start off against Indianapolis County Day Academy this year, but you've got to be looking toward the middle of the season, when you take on Madison County, South Side, and the big rivalry with Cathedral—"

"Stu," McPherson broke in, "I know this sounds clichéd, but we take each game, each opponent, one at a time. We've got our attention focused on getting football ready and on beating Indy County Day. We lost last year, and that's because we weren't focused. If we play the way I know we can, if we coach these boys right, and if the boys take the field with confidence and singleness of purpose, then we may, and I can't express this hard enough, may—*may*, God willing—be playing for a title down in Indianapolis come December."

The reporter turned back toward the camera.

"Reginald McPherson and his Cranmer Colonels sound confident. And they should be, as the fourth-ranked team in Class 3A. Tomorrow we'll be talking to the team right behind them, number five, Cathedral. I'm Stu Waterman, channel four sports. Now back to the studio."

It was a familiar sight after the first day of two-a-days, Jomo thought: tired players gulping water, drenched in sweat. Unlike the year before, Jomo felt good and pumped, amped and tweaked. He'd reached his goal: He was a solid 185 pounds— big arms, tight core, thick legs. He was down to ten percent body fat. Hell, he was ripped. He'd been off the juice for three weeks to clear out his system for the drug test, which he'd taken two weeks ago. He had some migraines, but his body had gotten back to normal when he'd started a new twenty-one-day cycle a few days ago. He wasn't worried about being caught; he was convinced by Ganz's assertion that his designer steroid was too hard to detect by some "Mickey Mouse lab looking for the obvious."

Early that morning the team ran. They did quick-step ladder drills—hopscotches, ins-and-outs, lateral foot drills. They jumped over blocking dummies, darted around cones, and did burpies until they dropped. They sprinted down the track doing fartleks—sprinting forty yards, jogging twenty yards, sprinting forty more, jogging twenty. Then again. They switched distances. And again. And again. As a final reminder that summer fun was done, they finished the morning dashing up and down the small embankment behind one of the end zones. Suicides, they called them. If they didn't run hard, the coaches would make them run more. But if they ran them right, the lactic acid brought about a burning sensation that bordered on the unbearable. There was no way to beat it. There was no place to hide.

The distraction from the TV station—the headmaster, trustees, boosters, all loved hearing and seeing Cranmer in a positive light in the media—seemed to cause McPherson to run the team to the edge. Jomo was surprised at how well the team kept up. Jeri's off-season workouts really did help.

After the TV crew left and lunch was done, the team donned helmets—no pads, according to state rules about wearing full equipment the first days of practice—and ran some more. They ran to and from stations where they worked on drills ranging from reading and reacting to one-on-one passing to tackling and blocking on the sleds.

"Oh, God!" cried a sophomore running back named Sean Drucker as he vomited behind the grandstands near the locker room.

"Breathe, kid," Jayson told him as he and Jomo hustled over. They waited to see if he was going to keel over. He didn't.

"Come on, kid," Jomo added encouragingly. Drucker

stood up, wiped his mouth, and tried to smile as if it was no big deal. But he was shaky, and his eyes betrayed him.

"Don't worry," Jayson told him with an evil grin. "Tomorrow is going to be far worse." Drucker groaned and trotted back to the field.

"Wash your mouth out before you put in your mouthpiece," Jomo yelled. Then he turned to Jayson. "He's supposed to be the next you."

"In his dreams, brother," Jayson said, laughing.

And the next day *was* worse. More hills, more fartleks, more agility drills. They added sled time, tackling dummies, blocking technique—all the things that simulate but, for Jomo at least, didn't stimulate. He couldn't wait to get the pads on and show off. And everything was at a faster pace. More blood, more bandages, more frayed nerves as players barked at one another, challenged each other. Thankfully, due to rules concerning hydration, no heat stroke. McPherson was a fanatic about hydration. Coaches kept charts on it. That's just what Jomo was doing, grabbing a crate of Gatorade from the utility closet by McPherson's office, when he heard the coaches talking about Jayson. He couldn't help himself—he stood stock-still to hear what they had to say. And, no surprise, Jayson was the talk of the camp, at least to Adrian Sims and Carl Burke, the team's defensive coordinator/defensive backs coach and offensive coordinator, respectively. It wasn't simply that he outran, outjumped, outhustled, and outshone everyone. The coaches agreed Jayson was the team leader they hoped he'd become.

He was the team's heart and soul. Jomo smiled, then he wondered what they thought of him. He heaved up the Gatorade as the coaches jawed about Trey's increase in strength but lack of mobility, Fitzie's speed and agility, and Calvin Reynolds's technique and drop in body-fat percentage. But just as he was about to leave, he heard his name. "And Rodgers—phew, that kid's grown up a lot since last year," said Sims. "Not just his attitude, but he really took to the strength training."

Jomo strained to keep from shouting a triumphant "Yes!"

"Proof's going to be when he puts on the pads and does some hitting," Burke said. Typical Burke, Jomo thought. That guy could frown on a free trip to Disneyland.

"I hear you, but you can just tell, you know," Sims said.

"And—," Burke started.

"And Coach Burke is old school—looking like a player ain't the same as being a player." McPherson laughed. "But I'm with Sims on that kid. This team is going to be good. If we don't win State this year—"

"What, Reg McPherson picking his team to win State out loud?" Sims interrupted. "I thought I'd never hear the day. You okay, Coach?"

"Yeah, I know Rodgers is good, but Jeri—," Burke started, but he was quickly interrupted by McPherson.

"Jeri what?" McPherson asked, which was exactly what Jomo was thinking.

"Jeri—" Burke cleared his throat. "She thinks something is going on with Rodgers."

What the—? Jomo wanted to scream. He'd passed the damn drug test; he'd been cleared to play like every other kid. What made his heart sink further was that McPherson didn't say a word for what seemed an eternity.

"When did she tell you this?" McPherson finally demanded.

"Yesterday, when we were going over some plans for conditioning drills," Burke said.

"She told you this *after* the drug screen came back?" McPherson said. "For Chrissake!" He must have called the weight room, because Jomo heard him bark, "Jeri. We need to talk. My office! Now!"

McPherson's door slammed shut. Jomo knew he should leave, but he felt bizarre, as if he had no feeling, as if his legs had been cut out from underneath him and he was floating. He realized he'd never, not once, given serious thought to what would happen if they found out. And what about Ganz? That really scared him—the thought of having to identify his crazy ex-skinhead dealer.

"Jomo!" He jumped and nearly sent twenty-four bottles of Gatorade crashing to the floor. But it was only Jayson, opening the door. "How long does it take to get some—" He stopped. "Yo, homes, I never thought I would say this to another brother, but you look like you've lost all the color in your face. You a'ight?"

"Umm, yeah, yeah," Jomo said. "I'm, umm, feeling sick," he said, before bolting past Jayson and into the bathroom.

• • •

It was a long, anxiety-filled night; the next day and night were worse. Jomo hadn't heard anything, and the fear that he was being watched and plotted against spooked him so much that he barely ate or talked to anyone. Just once he saw Jeri, who barely acknowledged his presence.

On the morning of day three, the team put on pads and the real hitting began. By the next day several sophomores were sent to JV, and three juniors—would-be scrubs anyway—turned in their pads and helmets.

By day five everyone had settled into a rhythm. In the afternoon the starters on the depth chart were called off to run official forty-yard-dash times. McPherson stood next to Sims, who held the stopwatch. Linemen went first—defense, then offense. The times ranged from the low to high five-second range. Calvin got a big cheer coming in at 5.97—lightning fast for him. Jomo was impressed, and so were the coaches.

"All right, big boy!" Sims yelled. "Speed *and* technique. It's coming together for you."

Next came the skilled position players. Fitzie and Trey ran in the second-to-last pairing. Fitzie hit the tape at 4.8 seconds, a tenth of a second slower than last year. Trey waddled by at 5 even.

"Boy, you're about as mobile as my dead grandmother," Sims shouted down the track. "Thank God you're a pocket passer."

"Yes, sir," Trey said, snickering. And that's when Jomo

realized what Sims was going to say next. It would be him . . . against Jayson, the only other player who hadn't run. His whole body buzzed with excitement.

And sure enough, Sims called, "Caldwell, Rodgers, on the line."

They glanced at each other, then settled into position: a standing start, but slightly crouched.

"Keep your mouth closed so my dust doesn't clog your mouth," Jayson joked.

Jomo didn't reply. He was ready, so ready, to show what he could do.

"On your mark. Get set. . . . Go!"

Jayson exploded off the line, arms pumping, chest thrust out. This was normal. What wasn't normal was Jomo keeping pace. He was actually keeping pace. He accelerated just as Jayson pushed past McPherson and Sims. A tie? Jomo wondered. He slowed when Jayson slowed. When they stopped, Jayson threw up his arms for a high five, but Jomo kept him hanging.

"Four point forty-eight!" Sims said, which was followed by *Whoas* and whistles. Even McPherson raised an eyebrow. Jomo grinned as Jayson patted him on the back.

"Dag, dog, when did you get fast?" Jayson asked.

"Secret weapon," Jomo said as they jogged back to the starting line. He'd finally held his own against Jayson. He couldn't believe it. This couldn't be just the juice. Juice didn't do it alone. He'd worked hard for this. Really hard. This was his.

"All right, I've seen enough," McPherson said. "No second run—everybody get back. Good job, you two," he said to Jayson and Jomo. Then he pointed at Jomo. "You're prime time—just like your buddy. Now keep it up."

Jomo felt himself blushing furiously, so much so that he looked down. McPherson's compliment had a second layer of meaning: Jomo couldn't be in trouble if McPherson was doling out compliments. He felt giddy. Jayson slapped his back again and whispered, "Way to go, brother." Jomo smirked.

Sims motioned Jomo over to him. "How much you weigh again?"

"One eighty-five," Jomo said.

"Kid, you're going to put the smackdown on some poor souls this year," he said, slapping Jomo on the shoulder. "Out-freakin'-standing."

Jomo swelled with pride. It was happening. They were starting to take him seriously. And by the time the first game came around, he'd be ready to get off the juice.

"Prime time," he yelled as he crashed into a blocking bag, nearly knocking an assistant coach on his butt. "Hell, yeah," he chanted as he ran to the end of the line of players. "Hell fuckin' yeah."

The team practiced just once on Saturday morning, a situational scrimmage. McPherson grabbed face masks and barked out reprimands after missed tackles and dropped passes. There was a lap for every fumble. Nothing new. But he was also seen slapping backs and butts and helmets and clapping his hands. Jomo broke up two pass plays and forced a fumble. He tackled Jayson for a loss, something that really got him going. He even got in a little trash talking.

"Slow your roll, homes," Jayson said, just moments before he broke three tackles and ran for a touchdown. Jomo fell to his knees as Jayson hustled back to the huddle.

"O great and powerful Caldwell, we're not worthy, we're not worthy," he joked. The coaches and players laughed. Even McPherson chuckled as he told Jomo to get up and back to work.

Earlier that morning, Jomo had woken up to his uncle Will bellowing about breakfast. His dad had left for a conference in New York, and Jomo was glad for the company. They talked football over eggs and toast.

"Heat stroke," Will guffawed, standing at the kitchen counter. "Back in my day, people thought that was for wimpy kids who couldn't take it."

Jomo chewed his bread and swallowed. "Yeah, well, McPherson's a maniac about it, so we're well hydrated and the coaches are constantly stopping to make sure we're not about to keel over."

Will shook his head. "Different age, different game."

"Not really. We still get licks in. They don't want us to let up too much."

"Hitting!" Will said, sopping up some over-easy yolk with his toast. "Phfft, man, shoot, you don't know hitting—"

"Here we go," Jomo kidded. "Our punter is six foot. Did you all even have linebackers that big?"

Will shrugged. "Six-foot kicker? Man, our kicker was what, like, six foot five, and he used to squat the cheerleading squad to build leg strength. That's how big our kicker was!"

Jomo smiled, because he knew the Will Rant was coming on: "Shoot. Come up in here acting like y'all are big and bad. Cranmer football. Home of champions. Puh-lease. In my high school, when we sacked the quarterback—"

"You took out his family, too," Jomo broke in. "Old rant. Stolen rant."

Will chuckled, took a bite of his eggy toast, and sucked down some coffee. Jomo looked at the sports page, checking last night's baseball scores.

"Yo, I forgot to tell you, I need you to close up tonight," Will said, punching himself in the chest to move up some gas.

"Regular time?"

"No, a little bit later. There's a neighborhood association meeting, so you'll have to close up by like nine thirty, maybe ten," Will said.

"Can't. I got a date," Jomo said, shoveling more eggs onto his plate.

"Sorry, but I don't have anybody else, plus I've let you slide for a couple of weeks for football."

"I don't think so—," Jomo said under his breath, shaking his head.

"Say what?"

Jomo stopped eating. He dropped his fork on his plate. "Uncle Will, come on—I haven't seen Miranda all week," he said firmly. "I'm wiped. I'd like some time with my woman. I'm giving you my time—"

"Whoa, whoa, whoa . . . giving?" Will looked at Jomo as if he hadn't quite heard what was just said. "You're getting paid."

"Whatever—"

"No, not whatever," Will said. "I'm not asking you, I'm telling you to close up tonight."

"Why can't you do it?"

"That's not the point, Jomo," Will said, standing up from the table to get another cup of coffee. "I'm having dinner with a contributor. She's interested in pouring more money into the center. I can't be there, and so you need to step up."

Jomo smirked. "Is pouring money a euphemism for you *getting some?*"

"Look, boy, you're my nephew and I love you," Will said, slamming the cup on the counter, splashing coffee. "But I don't know what's gotten into you over the last couple of months. You ain't cute and you ain't that funny. And if you ever say what you just said to me again, I will smack the black off you."

For a moment Jomo almost invited the opportunity to take on his uncle to prove a point—he was no longer little Jomo, and he wasn't afraid of anybody.

Will pulled the dishrag from the sink and swiped at the

counter angrily. Jomo watched him, realizing he'd gone over-board. But before he could say anything, Will wheeled around and stared his nephew down.

"I don't give a damn how big you get—don't ever think you're big enough or old enough to disrespect me."

"I'm not trying to disrespect you—"

"Jomo, just have your butt at the club tonight and close the place," Will said, throwing the dishrag back into the sink. He stormed out of the room.

Jomo tapped his foot under the table. Yes, he was in the wrong, he thought, but he didn't deserve his uncle's tongue-lashing. He pulled out his cell.

"Hey, babe, I'm going to have to work," began his message. "I've got to close up late, so let's have dinner and movie at the club?"

The day dragged on as the cold war continued. When Jomo showed up early for his shift, he and his uncle skipped their regular basketball game. Jomo simply checked in. For the rest of the day, Jomo and Will answered each other in mono-syllabic words. *Yes. No. I don't know. Nothing. Okay. Fine.*

But the day wasn't a total loss. Miranda not only under-stood that he had to work, she brought over a huge pizza—his favorite compromise, half pepperoni with green pepper and half mushroom pizza. They ate in the teen lounge. The build-ing was deserted except for the dozen or so people attending the neighborhood association meeting on the second floor.

Miranda listened while Jomo complained. While she didn't come out and take sides, she reminded Jomo that Will had often worked around Jomo's schedule.

"But I always made the time up," he said as they sat, knees together, on the couch.

"Yes, I know that, and he knows that, but he was in a bind, and he is your boss as well as your uncle," she said.

"So you think he's right?"

"I think you need to understand where he coming from. He needed your help," she said, reaching for a slice of mushroom.

"Yeah, well," he groaned.

"Plus, the crack about 'getting some'—bad, really bad. You kinda owe him an apology."

"He took it the wrong way."

"What is the right way here?"

"Uh, in the way it was intended—a joke," he said, lying back on the couch. He noticed his mouth going dry. "Damn. Y'all need to get a sense of humor."

Miranda dropped her half-eaten slice into the box and stared at Jomo.

"Now you're mad at *me*?" she asked. "You wanted to know what I thought, and I told you."

"Sheeeeet, baby, why you gots to act dat way?" he asked, deliberately trying to ramp down the tension.

She smirked. "Oh, no, you just didn't try to sound like you were mocking me," she said.

"Uh-huh," he said. Then he leaped on her and started tick-ling. He tickled her belly through her blouse, then high on the back of her thigh.

"Stop," she squeaked, squirming. "Stop."

"Say you're down with my mack," he said.

"No," she cried. "No. Never."

"Say it," he said.

"Okay," she said, and Jomo stopped. "I'm . . . down . . . with . . . you weak—"

Jomo tickled more furiously now. Miranda held out for a few seconds, but finally succumbed.

"I'm down with your mack!"

"Now who's your daddy?" he said.

"Stop! Stop!"

Jomo quit tickling her and pulled her into his arms. Miranda tried to catch her breath.

"I really, really l—," Jomo said, before shutting his mouth. Too soon, he thought.

"You what?" she said.

"I'm in deep like, deep, deep," he said. "You know what I mean?"

"Yeah," she said, touching her lips to his. He pressed into her, and they lay back on the couch. First vertically, then hori-zontally. Jomo unbuttoned her blouse enough to reach in.

"Isn't there a rule about doing this kind of thing at a boys and girls club?" she whispered.

"There's nothing posted," he said. He kissed her gently, and after a few minutes he let his hand drift down to the crotch of her shorts. Miranda stopped his hand. Jomo tried again, this time with a little more force.

"Jomo," she whispered. "I can't—"

"I know," he whispered, then moved his hands back to her waist.

But when she let him open her blouse even more, he couldn't stop himself; he tried again. He didn't let her squirming keep him from tugging the buttons on her shorts. Miranda blunted his move by grabbing his wrist and sinking her nails into his arm. And suddenly they weren't kissing. They were wrestling.

"Dammit, stop," she demanded, her face flushed with anger.

But Jomo kept yanking at her shorts, and she kept fighting until the button popped off. Miranda punched Jomo in the side of his head. He stopped and jerked away.

"I'm sorry," he muttered, as if he were trying to piece two parts of his mind back together—his own Jekyll and Hyde moment. "Oh, God, I'm sorry."

Miranda didn't say anything. She quickly buttoned her shirt, then looked for the button to her shorts. Jomo tried to help.

"Leave me alone," she snapped.

"I'm sorry. Miranda, I'm so sorry. Please," he pleaded, try-ing to hug her.

"Stop," she said, pushing him away. "I don't want to hear it."

"It's not me." And looking at her wild eyes, he knew he had to tell her. "It's this shit that I'm taking," he said, reaching out to hold her. She shoved him away, backing toward the door.

"I should've never taken that shit!" he pleaded. "I told Ganz! I told him . . . the steroids were screwing with my head. I'm sorry. That's not me."

"Steroids? What are you talking about?" she shrieked. "You attacked me."

"I know," he sobbed. "I'm so sorry. Please forgive me. You know that isn't me."

"Steroids! I don't know who the hell you are," she shrieked even louder. "You tried to . . ." She stopped to spit out the word. "Rape me."

"But I stopped—"

"*I* stopped you!" she bawled, thumping her chest. "I did! You bastard. I did it, not you."

Miranda was shaking; her mascara ran. Jomo tried to walk toward her.

"Don't," she said, holding an arm out. "Don't! Don't fucking come near me."

"Please, I'm so sorry," he begged again, folding his hands in front of him.

Miranda shook her head and ran out of the room. He followed.

"Miranda," Jomo whispered, but she was already out the front door. All that came in reply was the sound of the building's door slamming shut.

● ● ●

The minute the neighborhood association meeting was over, Jomo hustled the people out of the building, locked up, and ran all the way home. He broke down when he got there. He thought about going for a drive. But once he got in the car, he couldn't move. He just sat in the driveway and cried. Was this 'roid rage? What if she hadn't stopped him? And saying it meant that she was right—he wasn't going to stop. He wasn't. Going. To. Stop. It was almost surreal. He *knew* he'd done what he'd done, but he couldn't believe, he really couldn't believe he was capable of doing something so perverse, so monstrous. It was the steroids, it had to be the steroids. Or maybe this had always been inside him. He tried to stop them, but other thoughts flooded through. What if she told someone? Would they come and get him? And even as he wrestled with this new worry, he was aware of how selfish he was to be worrying about himself instead of Miranda. He was evil. . . .

"Fuck me!" he screamed, pounding the steering wheel. "I hate me. God, please kill me. Please kill me. I'm too much of a pussy to do it myself."

Eventually, he dragged himself into the house and locked himself away in his bedroom. He didn't talk to a soul for the rest of the weekend. He dared not call Miranda. She didn't call him.

The only person he did talk to was Ganz when the call came in on the cell. Ganz was in a great mood, as business was going well, particularly off some of the kids Jomo had sent his way.

"Rich kids," Ganz said, continued blabbing, not giving Jomo a moment for a word in edgewise. "I love rich kids. They don't complain about rates, and they bring me crisp bills. Damn, I'm lovin' it."

"Listen, I'm thinking about laying off," Jomo said the moment Ganz gave him a chance to speak. "I'm where I need to be. I don't need any more."

There was silence on the phone.

"Look, I gotta know, did you change the formula?" Jomo continued.

"So *that's* what's this is about." Ganz sighed.

"I just feel different. Really different," Jomo said.

"It's not my stuff," said Ganz.

"Well, it's not me," Jomo said.

"How do you know?" Ganz said.

"I know me, motherfucker," Jomo said, anger bubbling to the surface once again. "You don't, and I'm not so sure that you haven't been lying to me about the side effects."

"What did you call me?"

"Are you deaf?" Jomo said. He was pissing Ganz off and he didn't care.

"Well, well. Look who's grown up enough not to be scared anymore," Ganz said sardonically. "The way I see it, you've got a week of the shit left. You can call me at the service or not—I don't care. But you better keep your mouth shut. By the way, Jomo, ask yourself this: Is anyone else on the team, in the school, showing the same signs?"

The call went dead, but Ganz's question echoed in Jomo's mind. Trey hadn't seemed to change. Calvin . . . well, Calvin had developed an in-your-face attitude, but maybe he was taking football more seriously now that he was catching good vibes from the coaching staff. Football was intense to begin with, Jomo reasoned. But still, he felt different, and he couldn't know how anyone else was feeling, nor did he want to ask.

Jomo's supplies dried up six days later. At first he didn't feel anything. Not that he expected to—he hadn't gone through withdrawal symptoms when he'd stopped juicing for drug testing. On day two he got a headache so bad that he asked to go home. He slept horribly that night, so he felt even worse the next day, and the damn headache lingered on and off throughout the day. Thankfully, it didn't hurt most of practice. Still, every little thing pissed him off. He got so mad at Trey's mouth running during practice that he buried him into the turf during the team's red-zone drill. A shoving match ensued, with Jomo being told to sit out a couple of plays.

"You're hustling, but you need to save the rage for the game," McPherson told him. Still, he slapped him on the back and put him back into the drill two minutes later.

By Friday night Jomo felt his head was about to explode. He wondered if he should call a doctor. But then he'd have had to tell about the steroids. Plus he hadn't seemed to have the same problem when he went off to clear his system for the drug test. Was he addicted to the stuff? Thank God he had the weekend to recuperate. However, he got roped into a best-of-three rapid chess battle with his father, who had begged him to play after dinner. Jomo lost the first game quickly but worked hard for a victory in the second. The draw seemed sharpen his father's resolve as well as his tongue for the third game.

"You ready now?" he asked. Jomo slowly assembled the pieces. His head was pounding, and his father's voice was like daggers to his ears. "I guess you're full of yourself right now," his father growled happily. "It's just one game—don't let it go to your head."

"I'm ready," Jomo said, setting down the last pawn as his father rose and walked into the kitchen. He was back a few moments later with a tumbler filled with ice and, based on the smell from where Jomo sat, scotch. The good stuff, his dad called it.

"Do you have to . . ." Then Jomo caught himself. His father was clearly heading toward oblivion tonight, and what Jomo had to say on the subject wouldn't matter.

"Let's set the clocks for five minutes—blitz chess!" Edward barked.

The rules were complex, but the premise was simple: A player moves his piece as fast as he can and punches a timer after the move; then his opponent's timer starts running. The two previous games had been set at ten minutes, which was stressful enough for Jomo. Slicing half the time made Jomo crazy, because he didn't have the brain capacity for it—his head was filled with things far more complicated than chess.

"Fine," he sighed, rubbing his temples.

"Go," his father shouted, making his first move one second later. Jomo's mind went into overdrive trying to keep up, his father taking thirty seconds or less to make moves. Jomo did fine for the first couple of moves, but he could tell he was making mistakes, and was majorly pissed when he lost his rook and queen in the space of three moves. He thought harder and harder, his father putting him into check faster and faster, and dammit, he was faltering under his father's mastery yet again. Then he saw an opening. He snatched his father's queen and slapped the clock. He was surprised by the response.

"Round three to me," his dad bellowed.

"Wha? How?" Jomo's eyes rapidly alternated between the board and his father's face.

"Your knight made an illegal move in capturing my queen." Edward chuckled, shaking his head. "Moved four spaces rather than three," he added to rub it in.

Jomo's head throbbed. He tried to focus on his father's face. "You can't be serious!" he finally blurted out. "It was a mistake."

"You know the rules." His father continued to laugh as he picked up his tumbler and took a long, deep drink. "I win. If you had only focused—"

Before he could finish, Jomo stood up, picked up the chessboard, and threw it across the room. Pieces flew in every direction. Jomo stood stock-still, feeling completely unable to control himself. With his father staring at him as if he'd gone nuts, he fell back into his seat.

"I'm sorry—my head . . . my head is killing me," Jomo wailed. He could feel his heart racing, and then he felt his father's arms wrap around him. He couldn't remember the last time his father had hugged him, and he was overcome with an urge to tell him everything—the drugs, Ganz, Miranda, his rages. "I'm a mess, Dad," Jomo started. "I—"

"It's all right, shhhh, it's all right," his father whispered, holding him tighter. They rocked slowly together. "It's going to be all right, Jomo. I know you're under a lot of stress." Jomo heard his dad sniffle, then felt tears.

"We've put you through so much," Edward went on. "We've been so selfish, your mother and I. I didn't hear you. I'm here now. I promise, I'm here."

Early the next morning, his mother called to see how he was doing, clearly having been told of the incident. Jomo was surprised that his father had actually called her. He told her his headaches were better, and yeah, yeah, he would go to the doctor if they came back. And at the back of his mind, his darkest corner, he wondered what his mother would say if she knew the truth. Not just the steroids, but Miranda. She would never forgive him.

After their talk, Jomo left a message for Ganz. He wanted more; Ganz obliged. Jomo couldn't help himself. He knew he was addicted—at least that's what he was able to self-diagnose for himself from websites.

●●●

The weeks went on and the team came together. They focused on Indianapolis Country Day, their first opponent. School was scheduled to start the Monday following the Friday-night opener—no homework to worry about. At practice the Colonels' scout team, wearing white pullover mesh jerseys—pinnies—ran Indy Country Day's offense, an option attack with short passes with the quarterback on the run. The starters wore black pinnies. Both quarterbacks wore yellow—they couldn't be touched.

Jomo lined up in his safety position, but close to the line, anticipating a run play by Drucker, the sophomore, who, despite having a bit of a mouth, had caught the attention of coaches at practice. But his move from freshman football to varsity wasn't going to be easy if Jomo had any say about it.

"Set," Trey yelled from under center. "Hut . . . hut, hut."

It was a toss sweep to Drucker, who was patient enough to look for a seam. He found one, cut back against the play, and blasted through. Fitzie took a good angle, still, Drucker juked him. But then Drucker came up against a surging Jomo. The sophomore lowered his shoulders faster than Jomo did. The two collided, and Jomo went flying. Drucker's legs instinctively continued to pump, and he churned out another five yards before stumbling toward the ground. He gained a first down. Drucker bounced up and slapped the football.

"Good run, Drucker," Coach Burke yelled. "Way to drive those legs."

"Pick it up, Rodgers" was all Sims said.

"Can't catch me!" Drucker said as he dashed past Jomo. What a punk, Jomo fumed. The punk needed to be taught a lesson.

The second play from scrimmage started to look like a pass. However, Jomo sensed that Drucker was moving not to block, but for a short pass over the middle. True enough, everyone else on defense bit. Drucker caught the ball a few yards past the line of scrimmage, but as he turned to run, Jomo drilled him with a helmet-to-helmet collision. The sound ripped the air. Drucker's helmet popped off and bounded around the field. Jomo drove harder into Drucker's body, lifting him off the ground, and then pounded him into the turf. Jomo jumped up and stood over Drucker. He didn't notice the boy's eyes were closed. "I caught you!" Jomo wailed. "I own you! I own you!"

He trotted back to the defensive sideline feeling awesome. He'd popped people hard before, but this year he could tell his hits were vicious. He felt like he could have snapped Drucker in half.

Jayson grabbed the back of Jomo's jersey.

"What?" Jomo asked, swinging around and pulling away.

Jayson shook his head and growled, "You creamed the kid. . . ." Jayson looked over at Drucker. "Oh shit, he's still down."

With that, he bolted over to the huddle forming around

the sophomore. Jomo took off after him. Drucker lay there, eyes closed, not moving.

"Everybody step back," the team trainer said as he broke open smelling salts under Drucker's nose. That woke him up. He seemed groggy. The trainer checked him out. Drucker said he could feel and move his toes and fingers, then his legs and arms. He'd forgotten what day it was. He did know he was on the football field. As he tried to sit up, he vomited all over himself and began to hyperventilate. Jomo stared in horror.

"We need to get him to the hospital," the trainer told McPherson. "Possible concussion. I'm going to call an ambulance; I don't want to mess around."

McPherson nodded and thrust his cell phone into the trainer's hand.

The players retreated hesitantly to the sidelines, many of them taking a knee with their helmets off. A few prayed. Jomo looked around, stunned. He trotted over to Jayson, who was standing with his helmet half-on, half-off.

"Not now, man," he told Jomo.

Then Jomo noticed that no one would look at him. Screw 'em, he thought. Not his fault if the kid couldn't take a solid hit. But he couldn't pry his eyes away from the huddle on the field and, later, the ambulance that made its way toward them.

The attendants carefully slid Drucker onto a gurney, then rolled him toward the ambulance. Jomo's teammates clapped

Drucker off the field and shouted encouragement. Drucker gave a thumbs-up before they put him in the ambulance.

McPherson called practice. Everyone was dismissed, but as the players filed past him, McPherson said, "Rodgers, my office."

Jomo stood helmet in hand while McPherson tore off his ball cap and threw it to the corner. His face was red and his body tight. Jomo knew he was about to get blasted. He decided to make the first move.

"Coach, I know it was helmet-to-helmet, but I—I didn't mean it. I wasn't going for his helmet," he said, pressing his hands against his thighs to keep them from shaking.

"I'm going to ask you a question and I want the truth," McPherson said, his voice steely. "Are you juicing?"

"What?" Shit. Holy shit! Did he know? Was he guessing?

McPherson got in Jomo's face, backing him into a bookshelf. Jomo blinked repeatedly, opened his mouth to respond, then closed it again as McPherson bellowed: "Are you juicing—yes or no?"

Jomo's mind raced. He could tell him the truth. Everything. Right now. Take the punch. He'd be thrown off the team, probably out of school, but he'd be clear, right? He'd done Miranda wrong, he'd put Drucker in the hospital. But, dammit, no! He'd worked so hard to get here. He was so close. He could figure out a way of weaning himself off the stuff. It was all in his head, right?

So he said "No," shaking his head. He didn't know where it came from, like an involuntary action. "No, sir," he said again. He was surprised by the conviction in his voice.

McPherson stood back, searching Jomo's eyes. Jomo met his gaze.

"You've got to control yourself, son," McPherson said. "You could've hurt that kid. I've got no room on my team for someone who's reckless."

"Yes, sir," Jomo said. "I apologize—"

McPherson didn't acknowledge him; he walked out of his office and slammed the door. Jomo stared at the floor. Now he'd really screwed himself. He'd hurt a player, Jayson was pissed at him, and he had lied to his coach. But he had a chance to make it up. He just had to keep a cool head and stay out of trouble. He did a quick mental calculation. Three months of football meant, really, just two more months of the junk. Then he could quit. Jomo hurried out his coach's office and headed to the locker room.

He noticed a folded note shoved into the grille of his locker. "Yo, fuck face, we don't need you."

Jomo couldn't tell who wrote it, but in his mind it might as well have been the whole team. He crumpled it up and threw it into his locker. He slipped out of his jersey and pads, dropping them to the floor. But before he could sit down, McPherson appeared.

"Come with me," he said in a somber tone. Jomo caught his breath—what he saw on his coach's face was wide-eyed fear.

• • •

"Oh, I want her fired, do you hear me?" Jomo's father yelled at the headmaster, Dr. Campbell, and the head coach. He stood behind his son's chair, his arms firmly gripping his son's shoulders. "I don't know what kind of racist bullsh—" He stopped himself short. "This is my son's reputation you're messing with," he resumed, his voice more controlled. "I'm going to have this."

Jomo sat, not moving a muscle, madly trying to sort out what he should do. As best he could figure out, his father had gotten the call from Jeri not long after Jomo knocked out Drucker. She'd heard about Drucker and decided she couldn't keep her suspicions suppressed any longer. McPherson wouldn't take her seriously, so she'd gone to his dad. His dad had then driven from his office across town, burst into Dr. Campbell's office, and begun ranting. Dr. Campbell, caught completely off guard, had summoned McPherson, Jeri, and Jomo to his office.

Jomo wondered if anyone had ever spoken to McPherson the way his father was. Even Dr. Campbell and the members of the board of trustees didn't raise their voices to the man. But Jomo knew his father didn't care about the history and didn't have the reverence.

"She's accusing my son of taking steroids!" his father yelled, pointing toward Jeri at the end of the conference table. He wouldn't look at her. Neither could Jomo. One look and she'd know. And he knew that he should say something . . . but . . .

but . . . how could he? How could he, with his father standing right there, standing up for him? What would he think if he found out Jeri was right? There was no proof, he reminded himself. Jeri was making guesses—she couldn't prove a thing. He calmed down a little.

"My son—on steroids! I've seen him working harder than I've ever seen, do what he was asked, and this is what he gets in return—circumstantial evidence from Miss Thang over there."

Jomo peeked over at Jeri, who was still in her workout clothes. She sat stone-faced. Whatever she was thinking, she wasn't giving it away.

"Mr. Rodgers, please, let us try to keep this civil," Dr. Campbell implored.

"Civil!" Rodgers barked. "If somebody accused your son of taking steroids, would you be *civil*?" When no one responded, he added, "No, you wouldn't be. You'd be looking to kick somebody in the ass, that's what. Racist bastards. I should call my lawyer—"

"Mr. Rodgers," Dr. Campbell pleaded, "we don't need to go there. We can work this out."

The conversation didn't last much longer. Jeri and Jomo were sent from the office to the anteroom. The secretary was gone.

"I'm—," Jomo started to say, but Jeri ignored him and stormed out. Jomo sat down and wished he could go back in time. His conscience got a hold of him. It was all over him, making him think not just about what he'd done but who he had screwed along the way. *Come on, man, pull yourself together. You're so close*, he thought.

His father suddenly rushed out of the headmaster's office. "Come on, Jomo, it's time to go." Jomo saw McPherson behind him, his hangdog face and slouched posture telling Jomo everything.

On the ride back home, Edward told Jomo what was going to happen. Jomo's father was assured that Jeri's files and notes were locked away in Dr. Campbell's office. And Jomo's father agreed that the reason for Jeri's departure would be kept quiet.

"Dr. Campbell tried to shake my hand," Edward quipped. "I left his ass hanging. I stood up for you because I believe in you," his father told him. "I—we—your mother and I, we brought you up to do right in the world. This is why I worry about you and Jayson. White folks, they'll take it away from you. You saw what they did to Will. They'd do that to you or Jayson or any other black kid in that school."

Jomo now wished he were dead. He was bullshit, and he was dragging his father down with him. He tossed and turned all night long. He'd cost Jeri her *job*. And he'd likely also permanently damaged her relationship with her godfather. When he did fall asleep, Jomo dreamed that he was an out-of-control monster—who grew and grew, his head hitting the ceiling, his arms bulging out of windows. It was one of those dreams in which you know you're dreaming, but you can't wake yourself up out of it. When morning arrived, he took a long, hot shower to clear his head. At first he skipped his dose. He ate breakfast, he watched SportsCenter, he watched a half episode of *Star Trek* on cable. He drank a Coke, then another. He packed his bag for school and got his bike from the garage. "Shit," he said, dropping his bike. He walked back into the house, pulled out the shoe box, and stuck himself in the gut.

At the team's meeting that day, McPherson told them that Jeri had left to "pursue a really good opportunity." There were mumbles and groans; Jomo wouldn't make eye contact with McPherson. But the coach went on to tell them news of Drucker's health that buoyed their spirits, especially Jomo. He had suffered a concussion, but he'd be cleared to play in a couple of weeks. Jomo almost wanted to cheer. Maybe the team wouldn't continue to blame him. Before he could talk himself out of it, he interrupted his teammates' claps to apologize.

"Guys, you know me," he said, standing and looking around. "You know that I'm not, you know, um, one of those guys who headhunts and tries to hurt people, especially a teammate. The moment got to me. I just want to play hard this year, for us, for this team. We've got a once-in-a-decade team here . . . and I got a little too psyched."

Jomo looked around the gauge a response. Most people's eyes were on him, a few, including Jayson, stared at the floor.

"So I just want to say that I'm sorry for yesterday. I want to apologize to you, and I will call Sean and his parents and apologize to them," he said. "I hope you and they can forgive what I've done. And I will accept any punishment—"

Jomo stopped for a moment to compose himself. He wasn't lying. He really did want to be flogged to make the pain go away.

"Dude, sh— Excuse me, Coach," Fitzie started. "Stuff happens, man. Colonels, let's play hard, but let's play smart. Let's save the pain for the opponents."

"Yeah," somebody yelled.

Later, after practice, Jomo called the Druckers as promised.

"It's part of the game," Drucker's father told him, much to Jomo's surprise. "Now go kick Country Day's ass."

Everyone seemed to be in a forgiving mood, but there was a definite disconnect with Jayson. He didn't say one word to Jomo through the entire practice, so Jomo deliberately sat beside him on the bench as he untied his cleats. He gently bumped shoulders with him. "Yo, man."

Jayson took his time untying his left shoe. He packed it neatly into his bag, then said, "I saw Miranda last night at the mall."

Jomo stopped in mid pull and waited for Jomo to continue.

"Hello," Jayson said. "Earth to Jomo. Earth to Jomo."

"I don't want to talk about it."

"Yeah, well, she was mad too, but she wouldn't say more than that you two had a fight. I mean, she won't even talk to J'Leesa—"

"Let it go, bro," Jomo said, flinging his shoes into his locker. Miranda hadn't told anyone! The relief was palpable. And yet he hated that he was so happy to hear that Miranda hadn't told.

"See, there you go, bro," Jayson said. "We used to talk about stuff, but now—"

Jomo's relief shifted to anger. "God," he said, "why don't we have a pajama party tonight and share our feelings?"

"That's not what I'm saying, Jomo."

"Then what are you saying?"

"You're acting like you're too big, too bad, and can't be bothered with anybody, including me."

"Oh, it's about *you*," Jomo said, pulling off his pants. He stepped out of them, balled them up, and threw them into the locker. "Well, I'm no longer your baby-fat running buddy," he continued.

"It ain't never been like that," Jayson protested.

"You just don't like it that I don't need you looking out for me," Jomo said, yanking a sweatshirt over his head. "Is that why you ran to Drucker when I laid his ass out?"

"What?"

"Is he your new boy?" Jomo continued, pulling on his blue jeans. "Is that why you left that shitty note in my locker?"

"What note?"

"Oh, don't act like you don't know, Jayson. Is that how you play it in the 'hood now—leaving notes instead of standing tall when accusations are made?"

Jayson grabbed Jomo by the arm and pulled him close.

"You better quit," he said, his head cocked and teeth clenched. "I don't know what the hell has happened to you. If being on varsity has gone to your head—"

Jomo yanked his arm down out of Jayson's grip. "Whatever, Captain. Are we done?" Jayson nodded, and Jomo slid on his flip-flops, slammed his locker shut, and left. The next day he moved to a locker far from Jayson's.

The loss of Jeri and Drucker didn't seem to affect the team, as they started the season that Friday night with a 52–7 spanking of Indianapolis Country Day. Jayson was the star of the game—as well as the *Star-Review*'s male athlete of the week—with a 267-yard, three-touchdown performance, which included a 60-yard touchdown run. They didn't use him in the fourth quarter, nor most of the other starters. Jomo had a relatively quiet night, although he was good for eight solo tackles, including one on a fourth-and-goal from the two-yard line. He was pretty pleased, but he knew he still had some work to do.

The team celebrated that night, but Jomo went home. He'd come up with a new MO, and it was simple: pare everything down, be as streamlined as possible—weight training, school, practice, home. He'd fit work in on the weekends, and once or twice during the week, taking a later cleaning shift that no one wanted, which would make his uncle happy. The way he figured it, if he could control his environment, he could control his outbursts. And it seemed to work. His schoolwork was good—no surprise. His play was stellar, and while, sure, there were a few inexplicable blowups over trivial matters, only one was embarrassing, only one he regretted. During a heated cross-examination during a debate in advanced speech class, Jomo threw his index cards and notes at his opponent. There were simultaneous laughs and gasps. Gardner immediately called the debate and sent Jomo to stand in the hall for a while to cool off.

"I don't know what to say," Gardner said to Jomo after class. "Passion is good, but that was way, way overboard."

"I know, I know," Jomo said, trying to put together a sympathetic narrative for his teacher to respond to. Pressure in football? No, that wouldn't work. Wait, Jomo thought. Perfect. His parents.

"It's my parents," Jomo said, his voice developing a tremor. He hunched his head into his shoulders. "It's so fucked-up. Oops, I'm sorry."

"That's okay," Gardner said. And Jomo knew he had him hooked.

"See, my mom's in Seattle, Dad's here," Jomo continued, stealing a sideways glance at Gardner's ruddy face. "They aren't talking divorce, but I know it's there. It's all I can think about, and I guess—I guess I just snapped."

And as Gardner's face shifted from annoyance to concern, Jomo let Gardner take over. "If you need to talk, Jomo, I'm here," his teacher told him. "But if there's another outburst like that, I'm going to have to talk to the headmaster. Okay?"

Jomo nodded his head and went back into the classroom to gather his books just in time for the bell to ring. Gardner wrote him a note. "Remember, Jomo, I'm here. . . ."

Jomo walked out and nearly laughed at how easy it was to lie his way out of anything.

Jomo stepped up his program. He ate by himself or, whenever possible, spent time in the library reading while snacking on meal-replacement bars. He wanted to hear from Miranda—he hoped he'd hear from Miranda—but he didn't. And he didn't dare call her. He couldn't figure out how to make it better with her, and it ate him up every time he thought about her. To help himself stay chill, he forced himself to think about all the asshole things he'd done. If he remembered them, he wouldn't do them again. He even took to injecting himself in front of the mirror. It became almost a subject of fascination, wondering if he could see someone or something—a demon, perhaps—controlling him. He'd gotten what he wanted—he was huge compared to last year. He was solid muscle and model perfect. There were times when he wanted to dig his fingernails into his skin and see if there was something more than flesh and blood inside him. Yeah, if he stayed hyperaware of what he was doing, he could handle just a few more weeks. But twice now he'd woken out of a dead sleep with a terrifying thought. What if even after he stopped juicing, he didn't go back to "normal"? What if Ganz had been right all along: In his desire to get big, he'd let it all go to his head? If he hadn't gotten big, would McPherson have thrown him to the curb long ago? Even in the debate fiasco, most people had laughed, and his teacher had told him to settle down and "respect" his opponent. Would that have been the reaction a year ago?

As the season went on, the Colonels raked up wins against some of the toughest teams in their class. The road trip to Cleveland for the National High School Gridiron Invitational, an annual event broadcast nationally (but tape-delayed) by ESPN and featuring six teams from the Midwest and East Coast, was particularly successful. The Colonels squeaked by Bishop Keller, a national powerhouse with not just Division I prospects but potential pros. It was an upset that got the Colonels national recognition—particularly Jayson, but also Jomo and Trey.

On the ride back home through the Ohio and Indiana countryside the next day, Jomo sat by himself. Everyone else was talking smack and whooping it up, recounting great plays. But Jomo felt completely separated from it all, and it confused him. He knew he should be elated. He longed to sit next to Jayson and just shoot the shit. They didn't do that anymore.

And something weird was happening: The more acclaim he got, the more he wanted to hide. This is what waiting for the day of reckoning felt like, what the sword of Damocles his dad talked about was all about, he thought, as the rest of the team burned electric around him.

18

Jomo was psyched as he laced up his Jordans. It had been a while since he and his uncle had played basketball. It was homecoming weekend, and the students had been given the Friday off. At eight and zero, Cranmer was now ranked number one in class 3A. In the *Star-Review*'s rankings of all schools in its coverage area, the Colonels were number two, ahead of schools with much larger students bodies. And tonight was the last game before sectionals; it was also for the conference championship, a title that had eluded the Colonels for the last six years. As fate would have it, they'd be playing Cathedral, their archrival, the number four-ranked team in 3A.

Jomo's dad was out of town at a conference; when his uncle heard that Jomo had the day off, he dropped by unexpectedly, early that morning, and invited Jomo to play an early game of hoops—shoot-around, really, nothing physical—and go out for breakfast—his treat, of course. Startled, Jomo crammed shorts and sneakers into his gym bag and headed out of his room. He was at the stairs when he remembered his shot. He ran back to his room and shoved the smaller bag into his gym bag beside his sneakers.

Jomo was glad for the court time and uncle-nephew time—he was near bristling with nervous energy. It wasn't just the game; it was also the potential for a run-in with Miranda—everyone from both schools would be there for this, so surely Miranda would. What would he say if he saw her? Would she dis him, ignore him, point and say "You know what you did to me"? He'd also be playing against Miranda's cousin, a running back. Did he know? Would he be out gunning for him? Jomo forced his brain to shift gears to the fun of the moment.

"You've got a big game tonight, so I'm going lay off you a little," Will said, bouncing the ball at the top of the key.

"So I have a shot at winning?"

Will laughed. "That's the only way, nephew." He dribbled to the left and hit a fadeaway jumper.

"Yo," Will said. "I just felt as if I needed to be a little like Magic."

Will backed into Jomo, but Jomo was ready and played loose enough to give himself some room to move out of the way if his uncle lost his mind and thought he was back in college. Instead, his uncle turned up and tried to hit a jumper. It clanked off the rim and ricocheted to Jomo, who snatched it out of the air and popped it into the basket. *That* felt good. He hit four more shots in a row.

"Dag, I'm going to start calling you Baby Jordan if you keep that up," Will said. At that Jomo threw up a brick, giving Will an opening to blurt out, "Now there's the old Jomo shining through."

Jomo laughed. It was a raggedy game—no pressure, no scorekeeping, just shooting. After twenty minutes his uncle said, "Yo, let's call it." He bent over and rubbed his knees. "Let's eat."

"Cool, especially since I'm winning," Jomo said, hitting a last fifteen-foot jumper. "But lemme shower first; I'll be quick."

The club's locker room was small, just two shower stalls and a dozen bathroom stalls. Jomo waited until his uncle started getting changed; then he locked himself into a stall. He took the pen from the shaving bag, screwed on the needle, and plunged it into his abdomen in one quick, practiced motion.

"Yo, where do you want to go?" his uncle suddenly called from just outside the stall.

Jomo twirled around, and the pen slipped from his hand. He scrambled to grab it, but it skittered along the tiled floor and out under the door.

Jomo pressed his head against the door. Shit. Shit shit shit. There was a long silence, and finally his uncle said, "Uhhh, what's this?"

"Can I have it back . . . please," Jomo said, forcing the words out. He was busted and there was no escape.

Will shook the stall door. "Get out here."

Jomo unlatched the door. "It's not what you think—," Jomo started.

"What am I thinking?" his uncle asked, veins bulging in his temple and neck.

"The doctor—"

"Bullshit!" Will roared. "Try again."

Jomo tried to grab the pen, but his uncle shoved him back into the stall. Jomo went careening off the stall panels and crashed into the back wall and onto the floor, just missing the fixture. He was flushed with fear and, oddly enough, relief. Is that insanity, he wondered, relief in the face of the biggest screwup in his life? That at last somebody knew? He sat on the floor, motionless, and waited, for what he wasn't exactly sure.

"Why?" his uncle yelled, holding up the pen. He whipped it against the wall, high enough to miss Jomo's head but close enough for effect. Jomo cowered.

"When did you start doing drugs? Answer me!"

"I wanted . . . to," Jomo stammered, "I wanted . . . I wanted to be big. That's why I started juicing—"

"Juicing?" Will interjected, Jomo noticing that his uncle's face went almost instantly from mad to confused. "Those . . . that," he said, pointing to the broken pen and cracked cartridge, "steroids?"

Will stood back and staggered out of the bathroom. Jomo slung on his shirt and hurried after him.

"I'm calling your father," Will said, searching through his

phone for his brother's hotel information. "Why doesn't he get a Goddamn cell phone like everybody else?" His uncle paused and looked at Jomo. "Why didn't we see it? She *was* right."

Jomo heard the echo of Jeri's voice from months ago telling him to take the time to do it right. Too late now. "Don't call him!" Jomo cried out. "Let me tell him."

"I can't trust you," Will yelled at Jomo. "Damn, the number is upstairs." He snapped his phone shut. "Steroids," he fumed. "God, I never—"

"Uncle Will, please, you've got to let me make this right," Jomo pleaded. "Let me be a man."

He searched his uncle's eyes, frantic, but all he saw was unspeakable fury. He tried again. "Let me have a chance to make this right, Uncle Will. Please."

"I can't believe I'm going to do this," Will said, "but— damn, I can't believe you want me to trust you after you lied to us. Now your dad looks like a fool. He went to your school and he raised holy hell . . ."

"I know, I know! I let the team down—"

"Fuck the team! You let your family down," Will said. "Did Miranda know about this? Is that why she left you?"

Jomo went mum; there were some truths he couldn't let get out. His uncle would never forgive him. Maybe to the point of actually hurting him.

"Let me make this right," Jomo tried one last time. "I can make this right."

He truly thought he could.

"You call your daddy, and you call your coach," Will said. "If you don't get to your father by tonight, I . . . I don't know what I'm going to do."

Jomo went home. He paced for a while, clutching the cell phone, his hands sweaty. His heart was pounding. By noon he still hadn't dialed either number. He decided to drive to clear his head and consider his fate. He fidgeted with the radio, finally giving up when he couldn't find anything interesting. He jumped lights by accident, nearly getting rammed by a bus. He slapped himself in the face and waved apologetically at the bus driver, who replied by flipping him off.

At one point he thought about driving as far as he could and never coming back. He'd often wondered what that would be like, to just drive until the gas gauge read "E" and there was no money. What if he went all Kerouac or Jack London? But as he thought through all of his options, he decided that he'd play this one last game. He couldn't leave the team in the lurch last minute like this. They were counting on him. That would be the most responsible thing to do, he decided. He'd go off in a blaze of glory, kick ass and take names, conquer Cathedral and make 'em all cry in his wake. And then he would talk to everyone. He would seek out Miranda, and tell her to tell everybody. Yes, that was it—cleanse his soul by having every-one pile on him.

"If I'm going to go, go big," he told himself as he pulled up to the stadium ten minutes late. He ran into the locker room past his coaches. He got the stink eye, especially from McPherson, but they didn't jump him. There was a buzz in the room, more so than usual. He got dressed, sans shoulder pads, and the team went out early to do their pregame stretches and walkthroughs. An hour before kickoff, people were already starting to fill the two-thousand-capacity stadium.

As Jomo was in a hurdler's stretch, McPherson strode by. "Late. You'll be running laps on Monday," he said.

Jomo looked up and McPherson winked.

As game time neared, the atmosphere grew electric in the locker room. They were suited up. Jomo sat by his locker. This was the last game he'd ever be in, and no one knew it. Over and over he asked himself why he hadn't just come clean.

Jomo felt a slap on his shoulder pads. He jumped. It was Trey. Jomo nodded and slapped Trey's thigh.

"It's our time, in our house!" Jayson shouted out. "I love this game! I love it! Let me hear your game yell!"

The sound was deafening. The team was pumped. Jomo felt like he needed his stomach pumped.

"Boys, let's gather round," McPherson called out. "Boys! Colonels!" he yelled and clapped. "On me!"

The thirty-five players, five coaches, two team managers, one trainer, and Dr. Hyde gathered in front of McPherson. Most took one knee; guys in the back of the group stood.

"Let's bow our heads and pray in the words that our Savior gave us," McPherson said as he too, got on one knee, doffed his cap, and bowed his head. Everyone joined hands, making

McPherson in an interview taped earlier today. And to be honest, I've known the man for twenty years, and I haven't heard him so, well, excited, if you can use that term to describe the old ball coach."

"Excited?" Waterman laughed. "Well, he's eight and oh for the first time since gas was below a buck fifty a gallon. Now *Star-Review* sports columnist Greg Hyatt joins us in the booth. Thanks for sitting in."

"Good to be here," Hyatt said. "Great night for football. Clear, crisp autumn night."

"Yes, and what a match-up we have between two of the more storied programs in Hoosier high school football," House said. "This is the seventy-third edition of the Cranmer-Cathedral game. And this year there's more at stake than the 'Baby Brown Jug.'"

"That's right," Waterman said. "The Colonels and Red Hawks are ranked number one and number four in class 3A. My question to you, Greg: Is this game more important for Cranmer in terms of going into the sectional playoffs with momentum?"

"Yes," Greg began. "Cathedral is the only 3A team in the region that comes close to matching up to Cranmer's power and speed, a serpentine around the room. "Our Father," he

"Who art in heaven," the group said in uniso
be Thy name. . . ."

Jomo wasn't listening. He could hear the
laughing. He heard the monster whisper, in a s
voice, "Liar."

". . . the power, and the glory, forever and eve
McPherson stood up and put on his cap.

"I'm not going to give you some long-winded
said, his arms folded across his chest. "You know
to win."

He then unfolded his arms and leaned into h
jabbed a finger at them.

"Remember this: We don't get bullied in our
said, jaw tight. "Now let's kick these punks back h

With that the team roared and ran out of the l
and up to the tunnel. Jomo was the last to go.
walked behind him.

"You good, Jomo?" McPherson asked.

"Never better, Coach," Jomo said, slamming th
his padded forearm.

"Love it," McPherson replied.

"You're listening to Friday-night football on
WFWR-AM, 1260. I'm Phil House with the
play-by-play, alongside Stu Waterman.

"That was legendary Coach Reginald

led by junior Jayson Caldwell, who will, without
a doubt, be first team All-State. But Cranmer
isn't one-dimensional, with Trey McBride
really coming into his own as quarterback. He
has fourteen touchdown passes against
three picks, nearly a complete turnaround
in numbers from last year. The defense is
anchored by senior linebacker/co-captain
Casey Fitzgerald, a big hitter, as well as Jomo
Rodgers, an excellent run stuffer and good in
pass defense over the top.

"And with that crowd roar, here come the
Colonels from out of the tunnel."

The Colonels won the coin toss and elected to take the kick.

"And there's the kickoff, taken at the five-yard
line by Sean Drucker," House said. "He starts
off to the left with his blockers. Whoa—he cuts
back to the left and is taking off up the sidelines.
He's at the twenty, twenty-five, thirty, thirty-five,
forty. And he's hit out of bounds at . . .
let's call it . . . at the forty-eight-yard line. Man,
what a start to this game."

"This is Drucker's third game back after
suffering a concussion during a preseason
practice," Waterman said.

"First and ten for the Colonels on their forty-eight-yard line," House said. "Colonels come out of the huddle with two receivers: Jayson Caldwell lining up in the slot, with Drucker in the backfield.

"There's the snap, McBride, play action. McBride rolls left . . . set, fires to Caldwell, who's at the forty-five by himself and he's gone, folks. . . . Touchdown Colonels!"

"Jomo, Jomo," Fitzie yelled, dragging Jomo away. "Get your head in the Goddamn game, man." Jomo had missed an easy pick. He was on Cathedral's side of the field. Instead of running back to the huddle, Jomo stopped and looked into the visitors' bleachers.

"I don't see her," he said as he trotted back.

"See who?" Fitzie asked, trying to talk over the crowd.

"Doesn't matter."

Jayson's touchdown was the only score of the first quarter, as the teams went back and forth, with good plays followed by dropped passes, overthrows, and sloppy play on both sides. Jomo was burned twice for long gains, both on missed tackles on running plays. He was saved both times by Fitzgerald's hustle; on the second one Fitzie managed to strip the ball out of a Red Hawk running back's hands.

Cathedral got on the board early in the second quarter,

when Trey was hit from behind on a blitz and coughed up the ball on the Cranmer twenty. One of the linemen picked up the bouncing ball and rumbled into the end zone.

Mercifully, the half ended with the score tied at 7.

The third quarter got worse for Cranmer, specifically for Jomo. On the first play from scrimmage Jomo bit on a fake run. He moved up too far—and watched one of the defensive backs get smoked for a thirty-five-yard pass play down the sidelines. If the receiver hadn't had to turn and come toward the ball, he would've made it to the end zone.

Jomo smacked himself in the helmet. "Come on, dammit! Get in the game," he swore at himself.

Fitzie slapped him on the back of the helmet in the huddle. "Come on, guys," he told his teammates. "Come on, stick to the game plan. Play smart," he said again before calling the defensive play.

On that next play, Jomo was made to look even more foolish. Cathedral's star running back blocked down for a two count on a rush and then slipped out into open space, where he caught a five-yard swing pass. As he turned upfield, the back got a good block by the tight end on Fitzgerald and now only needed to get by Jomo, who—crap all—was out of position again. He started running for everything he was worth.

"Allen is moving upfield with only Rodgers
to beat," House said. "Allen . . . oh my gosh,
what a spin move, and he just froze Rodgers.

Allen's at the thirty . . . twenty . . . ten . . .
touchdown. Cathedral goes up 13–7. And
Katie-bar-the-door, we've got a barn burner
tonight."

All Jomo could do was scream, "Shit, fuck, shit." The language hacked off the ref.

Jomo resisted the urge to curse the old coot out and stormed over to the sidelines. McPherson didn't say a word, but Burke grabbed him by the shoulder pads. "You know better," he bellowed, pointing at his temple. "Think."

Jomo stalked off, banging his helmet on the metal bench and kicking a water jug. Fuming, he sat down.

"Don't get too down, man," Jayson said, holding a fist out. "You've got to go back and shut 'em down, man."

Jomo shook his head and bumped knuckles. It was the first time he'd shared a moment like that in weeks with Jayson. And he couldn't help but wonder: Was Jayson being a captain when he'd come over, or was he being a friend?

Cathedral blew the two-point conversion, with Fitzgerald tipping away a low pass to a Red Hawk receiver. Jomo jogged back to the sideline, where he was met by Sims, who berated him for the cardinal sin of leaving his feet in a tackle from the front.

"You looked like a damn flying squirrel out there," Sims shouted.

McPherson came over and bawled Jomo out. "You've played football for three years here, and that was a mistake that freshmen don't make this late in the season." His eyes were stormy under the brim of his hat. "Get your mind in the game."

Jomo slapped hard at the breastplate of his shoulder pads. "Come on, man. Come on. You can do this." He smacked himself one last time and settled down to watch.

In the next series of plays Jayson was, for the most part, Cranmer's offense. The coaches called his number eight times, including a toss sweep around the right side of Cathedral's struggling defense that led to a touchdown. The kick was good, and Cranmer reclaimed the lead.

Jomo headed back into the game after the kickoff. Cathedral had again gotten good field position just inside Cranmer's territory. On the first play from scrimmage, Cathedral tried the same play that they'd scored with earlier in the quarter, as Allen slipped into the left flat and received a pass. He juked past some Cranmer players and took off up the sideline. Jomo took off after him, feeling like he'd just downed rocket fuel. . . .

"Rodgers is closing in. . . . Allen moves to outside Rodgers. . . . Oh, he—"

Jomo wrapped his arms around Allen's throat and drove him headfirst into the turf. The force was so hard that Allen's body rolled up over his shoulders and the boy flipped over sideways.

He didn't move. Jomo popped up off the turf, looked at the Cathedral sidelines, then pointed at Allen. "Don't try that shit again!"

"Now there's a melee, with Red Hawks spilling off the bench onto the field, going after Rodgers," House shouted hysterically. "I can't believe this. Several of the Colonels' defensive players are trying to hold Rodgers back. What? What? Oh, players from both teams are running onto the field. I don't see Allen. I don't think he's up."

"And did you catch Rodgers?" Waterman said. "For some reason, he was pointing and yelling at Allen after the tackle. I think he even yelled something at the Red Hawk bench. It was an unnecessarily rough tackle, but the taunting was worse. There's no place in the game for that—that—unacceptable behavior. Completely out of line."

House broke back in. "The referees and coaches are holding the teams back—and I see a trainer and some Cathedral coaches tending to Allen. My producer is signaling that we need to take ten-second station break. Hold on—no, we're staying here for the moment."

"Folks, if you missed it, we've had the strangest set of, I don't know what you'd call it, actions, that I've seen since I've been in the booth," House said coming in from the break. "First, Jomo Rodgers, Cranmer's free safety, brought down Cathedral's Michael Allen with a vicious tackle—grabbing Allen around the neck and just driving him into the ground. Then Rodgers started taunting Allen and the Red Hawk bench. We've got word from the officials that Rodgers has been ejected, and his actions, both personal fouls, result in Cathedral getting the ball first-and-goal at the ten-yard line. And . . . hold on a minute. . . . They're calling for a stretcher for Allen, and this kind of injury could be serious, folks."

"That tackle," Waterman said pensively. "I think he meant to hurt Allen."

"I know that's not the kind of football Cranmer plays, Stu, and Rodgers isn't known for being a headhunter," House said. "But . . . I don't know. This is just a terrible thing to have happen in what was shaping up to be a great game."

"I don't want to see you in the locker room when the game's over," McPherson said, his voice low, dangerous. "Get out of here."

No one said a word to Jomo as he shuffled away from the sideline and toward the tunnel. He heard boos—from the Cranmer sidelines. When he reached the tunnel, a voice called out, "Hey, Jomo, what happened out there?"

Jomo turned. It was Greg Hyatt, the prep sports columnist at the *Star-Review*. Normally Jomo would have been psyched to talk with him, but not now. At first he thought about flipping him off. Instead, he turned back around.

"What . . . what happened out there?" Hyatt asked again, chasing after Jomo.

"You want to know what happened?" Jomo demanded, his eyes wide as saucers. "I'll tell you what happened. I'm a fucking liar and a cheat, that's what."

"What?" Hyatt said in astonishment.

"Yeah, put that in the fucking paper," Jomo hollered. Then he started laughing. He couldn't control himself.

"Ask yourself how somebody puts on thirty-five pounds of solid muscle in eight months," Jomo said. "You get it now?"

Jomo looked at Hyatt and knew he knew. Jomo started running.

"Jomo? Jomo? I need you to say it."

"Enough with the questions," Jomo said, reaching the door. He ducked in and locked it.

"Is anyone else juicing?" he could hear Hyatt yelling through the door.

Jomo stripped out of his uniform, leaving everything in a pile. He threw on his sweatshirt and sweatpants and letterman jacket. Hyatt was waiting in the tunnel, which led out to the parking lot as well as the field.

"You're tight with Jayson Caldwell—is he juicing?" Hyatt asked.

Jomo shoved the reporter against a wall, grabbed him by the shirt, and said through gritted teeth, "You say or write some shit like that, I'll kill you. I swear to God I'll kill you."

He shoved Hyatt once more and bolted out of the tunnel. Flinging himself into his car, he gunned out of the parking lot, just barely missing another car.

As he sped through the streets, he was sure his head would explode from the barrage of thoughts banging like a thousand toy monkeys clanging on tin cymbals echoing through his skull. To add to the list of unconscionable actions, now he could add threatening to kill someone to the list. "Shut up! Shut up!" he screamed. It was at that instant that he ran through a red light and narrowly clipped a motorcycle. The next time, he thought, that would be it—God was going to get him. And with that, he felt a calm come over him. There was nowhere go.

He pulled out his cell phone. He hit #4 on his speed dial.

"Hi, this is Miranda, leave a message at the beep. Beep. Sorry, that's not the real beep. This is."

"I always hated that," Jomo said, forcing cheeriness. Then his voice turned serious. "I just called to say that I'm sorry. I can't think of anything else to say. I know that doesn't mean much. Oh, shit . . . the cops."

Jomo dropped the cell. He glanced into the rearview mirror. A cruiser was fast behind him, its red and blue lights flashing.

Jomo started to cry. He fumbled on the seat for his cell, then punched in 11—home. He realized that he was closing in on the Calhoun Street Bridge. He sped up. He banged his hand on the steering wheel.

"This is the Rodgers' residence. Please leave a message."

"Dad, please forgive me," he said after the beep. "I've screwed up so bad. I've hurt everyone."

The car swerved, and the last thing Jomo saw was a bridge abutment. "Forgive me," he whispered.

Part V

"FAME IS LIKE A RIVER, THAT BEARETH UP THINGS LIGHT AND SWOLLEN AND DROWNS THINGS WEIGHTY AND SOLID."

—Francis Bacon,
English philosopher and statesman

Jomo awoke to the sound of a heart-rate monitor. That was weird. And he felt cold, really cold.

He opened his right eye first, and it was as if his mind was peering through to someone else's life, a life that appeared to be smeared with jelly. He opened his left eye.

Two eyes were a little better, but not much.

He stayed that way, barely conscious, rousing himself to some semblance of alertness. He thought he should sit up. He realized he hadn't the slightest clue how.

Could he move his head? He tried, slowly turning it first to the left and then to the right, and tried to focus. He saw flowers and somber-looking cards and . . . his mother asleep on a chair.

That didn't make any sense.

He looked down and saw an IV tube in his arm. He slowly

looked up to the IV bag and monitor, which hummed along loudly enough to be annoying. He was in a hospital, but that didn't make any sense either.

He lay still, and images in his mind slashed away like jump cuts in a movie. Snippets of things, but he couldn't hold onto any one thought. His legs ached so much that he didn't want to try to move them. He pulled the covers down to just above his knees, and saw bruises everywhere. *Shit*, he thought. He suddenly felt queasy, but managed to swallow back the bile. He wanted to go back to sleep. As he began to nod off, he thought he heard his father calling him. He tried to smile.

"Dad."

His father hit the nurse button, then nudged Jomo's mother awake. The nurse ran in, then called into the hallway to have the attending physician paged to the room.

"Mom," Jomo whispered.

"Yes, baby, I'm here," she said. She was crying.

"He recognizes you, and that's a good sign," the nurse said, checking monitors and writing on his chart.

"Dad, why's Mom crying?" Jomo asked.

"You've been, um," his father started, trying to choke back his own tears. He cleared his throat. "You were in a coma."

"Coma?" *Seriously?* he thought.

"Thirty-two days," his mother said, reaching for his hand.

"I don't . . . How?" It was so hard to concentrate on words.

"You don't remember?" his father asked. "There was an accident—"

Jomo's mother shushed him. "Let's let the doctor talk to him first."

"I'll call Will," his father said, jumping up. "Jayson too."

"Yes, yes, Jayson," she said, stroking Jomo's hand. "He's been here every day. Sometimes he'd do his homework—" And she began to sob.

Jomo was having a hard time processing everything. But he smiled thinking of Jayson.

"Yeah, Jayson," he said, and felt himself drifting away until a bright light in his eyes snapped him to attention. A doctor was standing over him with a penlight. The intense beam in his eyes was annoying, but at least it didn't hurt.

"You're incredibly lucky," the doctor told him as he flashed the light from eye to eye. Mint. Jomo could smell mint on the doctor's breath. Then he could smell . . . nicotine. The twin smells swirled in his nostrils and further clouded his already random thoughts. Then he realized the doctor was still talking to him. He forced himself to focus.

"It's a miracle, really," the doctor was saying. "You have some lesions to your frontal lobe, but I've seen people get past far worse damage. You've got a good chance of recovering. There could be short-term memory loss, possibly long-term. But now that you're awake, we can run some more intensive tests, get started on therapy. . . ."

Jomo felt that he should respond in some way, but all he could think to ask was "Why do I want to sleep all . . ." He stopped; his eyelids felt so heavy. Every single part of him felt so heavy and drowsy.

"Like you want to take a nap all the time?" the doctor finished for him, putting his hand on his shoulder. Jomo nodded. "You're going to be like this for the next couple of days, but gradually, you'll be able to stay awake for longer durations. It's going to take some time before you get back to, well, normal. That was a hell of an accident you were in. You're lucky to be alive."

The doctor turned to Jomo's parents and motioned for them to step outside the room. Accident? Jomo wondered. What accident?

"Captain," Jomo called out as Jayson walked into the room a little while later. A half hour? An hour? A day? Jomo couldn't tell. But Jayson was here. Jayson laughed. They were alone.

"Jomo, man, I—"

Jomo tried to sit up. He felt like he was outside himself, watching himself try to do things. He was trying to wrap his mind around what his parents had told him. A coma. Thirty-two days. That was bad, *that* at least he knew. And the whole idea of being in a coma for more than a month was hard to handle.

And he suddenly remembered something, "Play . . . offs," Jomo asked.

"Yeah, dude, we're going to State," Jayson said. "We're

going down to Indy on Saturday. We're taking your jersey with us. I wish you could be there with us too."

Jomo nodded and squeezed his friend's hand harder.

"I know we're not supposed to talk about it," Jayson said. "But dude, you could have come to me. You can *always* come to me. It makes sense now, but—"

He stopped as Jomo's parents walked into the room. Jomo wasn't clear on what Jayson was talking about.

Recovery was a slow process. Most days Jomo lay in bed, frustrated, as his mind flashed pictures and words, letters and numbers. Beyond simple words and familiar names, he couldn't put it all together. And yet somehow he knew he should be able to. Conversations seemed to echo and whirl around in his head. The parade of teammates and classmates began during the week leading to the championship, and after that came teachers and coaches. Some flowers arrived signed by Dr. Campbell and members of the board of trustees. "Screw 'em," his father said as he tossed the bouquet in the trash.

"Dad . . . why?"

His father didn't respond, which pissed Jomo off. "Why?" he asked again, getting agitated. To his shock, instead of answering, his father hugged him. Tight.

McPherson showed up the Monday afternoon the Colonels won the title—Cranmer had given itself the day off. His visit was brief, and Jomo noticed that his dad barely said a word, and offered only the limpest of handshakes. His mom was more cordial. Jomo tried to concentrate on what the coach was saying, but his mind kept floating away and he'd lose track of the conversation. McPherson handed Jomo a championship medal. That he got. They'd won the whole thing.

Jomo gave his coach a thumbs-up. McPherson was stone-faced. He turned and walked out.

"Ganz," Jomo screamed, jolting up. He was coughing between gasps for breath. He searched madly for the emergency call button. But there was no call button. He was home.

"Ganz," he screamed again.

His parents ran into the room.

"Jomo, Jomo," his father said soothingly, holding Jomo's shoulders, trying to keep him still. His mother ran to get him some water. "Shhh. Shh. You're okay. You're home," his father told him.

His mom came back with the water. Jomo grabbed it and gulped. He remembered that he'd been home for a week.

"Ganz," Jomo said. "The guy I bought the—"

He stopped. And like a DVD on fast forward, it all came back: Ganz, Miranda, the bad craziness, his lies. In all the seemingly nonstop chatter that had flowed from his parents, it was the one thing they had avoided.

"Steroids," his father said hesitantly. "I know. Will told us. We've been . . . we've been . . . well, we were waiting for you to remember."

"We've been holding off some damn reporter from the *Star-Review*," his mother added. "He said you 'implied' something was going on—"

"Oh, God, there was a guy . . . a guy I hurt at the—"

"He's fine," his father said. "Broken collar bone and concussion. It could've been a lot worse."

"God, I'm such an asshole," Jomo said. He couldn't look at either of his parents. No more deceit, no matter the consequences. This was going to suck, he thought.

He forced himself to look back at their faces. His parents, who'd always trusted him, no matter what. He realized his father's eyes were clear. Sad, tired looking, but clear. His mother looked thin. Thinner than ever. He took a deep breath. "I lied to you," he continued. "I lied to Jayson, to Coach. I thought I was turning into a monster. I even hurt . . . Miranda."

"Miranda?" his father asked.

Jomo spilled it all—how he'd started buying from Ganz, and how, when the prices went up, he hipped some other people to Ganz. He told them how the shots made him feel: powerful, invincible, and for no reason vicious and predatory. He told them how he'd hurt people, how he'd meant to hurt Harper, Drucker, and the running back from Cathedral. He talked about how he couldn't control himself. Then, hardest of all, he went into detail about that night at the Boys & Girls Club. And as he knew they would be, they looked aghast. Shocked, even—yes, it was true, and how could they not be, because it was exactly how he felt about himself—repelled.

"I mean, Jomo, couldn't this have been, you know, a mis-interpretation of her actions and yours?" his father spluttered.

"No," Jomo said. "I was trying to rip her pants off. I didn't want to stop. She slapped the hell out of me, and we haven't talked since. I was hoping that maybe she called? Or sent something . . ."

He trailed off. His father shook his head. His mother was quiet. He couldn't tell what she was thinking. She seemed to turn to stone. Then she walked out of the room, and he heard her walk down the steps. The front door opened and closed.

Jomo buried his head in his hands.

The next afternoon Will brought in some chicken soup. He found Jomo staring out the window.

"They hate me, don't they?" Jomo asked.

"It ain't easy on them," his uncle said, holding out the tray. Jomo waved it away. "You and Miranda—that knocked your mom for a loop. She doesn't know what to say. She wants to believe it was the steroids messing with your system, but . . ."

"But?" Jomo said, and he felt as if his heart was breaking.

"But," Will said, looking, Jomo saw, at everything but him, "it's hard. They've got all that to sort out, plus Hyatt, the guy from the paper. He's been trying to talk to you since you woke up."

"Shit," Jomo said.

"I'll let you slide on that one, but you've got to stop with the cursing," Will said. Jomo gave a short laugh. He added it to the list of things he needed to work on.

"Anyway, your dad is getting it from the school too," Will continued. "That Hyatt guy called your coach after the championship. So Cranmer is hammering away at your parents, particularly your father. They want to know what you know. They believe your dad knew the whole time—"

"But that's not true!" Jomo protested.

"It doesn't matter," he said. "They're going to believe what they want to believe."

"I don't think I'll be playing football anymore," Jomo said.

"Well," Will said, shaking his head, "we'll see. The Cranmer folks, they don't want anything that'll put the stink on their shiny new trophy. Nobody is talking out loud, but there's a whole lot of whispering on the down low. What I've been told is that the paper wanted to run something, but because of the accident and the coma, the school convinced them to hold it until they had all the facts." Will looked glassy eyed.

On the shelf opposite Jomo's bed was the set of encyclopedias Jomo had won when he was ten in the library's summer reading contest. There was the collection of shiny participation ribbons, medals, and trophies from football, baseball, and chess. He looked at his well-worn books, novels, biographies, and histories. There was his "naked" comic collection: He detested putting them in bags. He looked at his closet, once a tragic territory where shirts and pants lay in heaps on the floor, now clean. *Thanks*, Mom. Jomo's shoes had always been carefully placed in the two-tier shoe stall the two of them had built for his Cub Scout woodworking merit badge.

"Whatcha thinkin' about?" Will asked.

"How I make it right," Jomo answered.

It was early morning, and Jomo and his father washed and dried breakfast dishes. His mother had gone for a run. Jomo was scraping at some eggs on a plate when he noticed his dad had stopped drying and was pinching the bridge of his nose as if to stop himself from crying.

"Dad," Jomo said gently. "What?"

"Why did you do it?" he asked. "That's what I can't figure out."

Jomo didn't know what to say.

"I'm just so confused," his father said, running his hands over his head.

"I think . . . I think I wanted to be somebody," Jomo said, sending the last bits of dried egg winging into the sink.

"You *are* somebody."

"Yeah, yeah, I know. But I wanted to be *somebody*. Do you know what it's like to have people kissing your ass—"

"I'm a professor."

Jomo laughed. His father smiled. It was so great to see a real smile on his father's face.

"It's not an excuse, but I just liked—no, I loved it—I loved the attention."

His father nodded, then took a deep breath. "Jomo." He paused, sighed, and began again. "I just have to know. Your mom . . . she . . . well . . . she says not to ask, but I've got to know. Did you mean to kill yourself or did you lose control of the car?"

Jomo started to answer, but his dad cut him off.

"Actually, you know what? Don't answer," his dad said. "You're going to have to get some counseling. We all are. Me and you. Me and your mom. All three of us."

Jomo nodded. He gave the plate one last rinse and handed it to his dad. And he knew it was his turn, for the one question he had for his dad. He blurted it out before he chickened out.

"So—why do you drink?"

"What?"

"Why do you drink? Not that I've noticed you doing it since I've been home."

"The truth?"

Jomo shrugged his shoulders in the universal body-language sign for "duh."

"Painkiller. Memory dampening."

"Mom?"

"I thought so at first. But it's not her and it's not you, it's never you! It's me, you know—"

The phone rang, and Edward picked up the portable sitting on the countertop. He listened for a moment, head cocked. "Look," he said. "How many times do I need to say it—he doesn't want to talk to you."

Jomo knew it had to be Greg Hyatt.

"Tell his side of the story," Edward scoffed. "It's the least well-kept secret in town. . . ."

"Dad," Jomo said. "Dad!"

Edward waved Jomo off.

"DAD!"

Jomo felt a sudden surge of adrenaline. He turned off the water and motioned for his father to give him the phone.

"Hold on," Edward told Hyatt. He shook his head at Jomo. "No."

"I'm going to do it, anyway," Jomo insisted. "You can't protect me forever."

"I can try." Edward covered the receiver. "These people . . . these people will come after you. I'm talking about what old money and city fathers and first families can do. I can't let you do this."

Jomo held his hand out. It was trembling.

"Right now," his father continued, "right now, you can transfer to South Side, go to summer school, graduate next year. Or—or you can go live in Seattle—"

"You hang up, and I'll call him on my cell, or I'll go downtown to see him face-to-face."

"He'll get his story, and the cops will come and they'll lock your ass up," his dad said desperately. "That what you want?"

No, that's not what he wanted. It was so not what he wanted. And he knew, he *knew* what would happen next. He was toast. But he was burned either way, and at least this way. . . .

"Dad, this way I can quit with the lies. I can't change what happened. I can only change what's gonna happen. And what's gonna happen is that I'm going to step up, I'm gonna face the damn music." His eyes stayed locked with his father's. He waited. He could actually feel the blood pumping through his veins. And without breaking the stare, his father took Jomo's right hand and placed the receiver into it. Turning on his heel, he left the room. A moment later Jomo heard the front door click open, then shut. He looked to the phone in his hand. It was slick with sweat, hot to hold.

"Hello! Hello! Mr. Rodgers! Are you there?"

"Hello," Jomo said in an odd squeak. Instead of tightening up, Jomo's body felt light, almost electric. He swallowed hard and tried again.

"Hello, this is Jomo."

FROM PULITZER PRIZE—WINNING NOVELIST
OSCAR HIJUELOS
COMES A STARK, GRITTY, AND UNFORGETTABLE JOURNEY

"Like Huck Finn and Holden Caulfield, *Dark Dude* is our street-wise guide to the universe, the outsider with a changing view of what it means to be inside. Oscar Hijuelos knows how to kick around the big questions: Who are we? Who do we want to be?"
—Amy Tan, *New York Times* bestselling author of *The Joy Luck Club*

FROM ATHENEUM BOOKS FOR YOUNG READERS
Published by Simon & Schuster

Imagine you and your best friend head out west on a cross-country bike trek. Imagine that you get into a fight—and stop riding together. Imagine you reach Seattle, go back home, start college. Imagine you think your former best friend does too. Imagine he doesn't. Imagine your world shifting. . . .

jennifer bradbury

Some friends fade away. . . . Others disappear.

shift

★ "Fresh, absorbing, compelling."—*Kirkus Reviews*, starred review

★ "Bradbury's keen details about the bike trip, the places, the weather, the food, the camping, and the locals add wonderful texture to this exciting first novel. . . ."—*Booklist*, starred review

"The story moves quickly and will easily draw in readers."
—*School Library Journal*

"This is an intriguing summer mystery."—*Chicago Tribune*

"*Shift* is a wonderful book by a gifted author."—teenreads.com

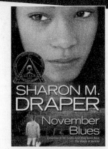